THE ARBORIST

P.T. PHRONK

The Arborist

Copyright © 2016 by P.T. Phronk

Cover and interior illustration and design © 2016 P.T. Phronk.

First edition (1.3)

Published by Forest City Pulp

www.forestcitypulp.com

CHAPTER 1

A tree appeared behind my house overnight.

When Amy and I first planned to move in together, I required that we find a place where I could live among trees. This house sat nestled at the end of a dead-end street, the last vestige of the suburbs before they gave way to forest and wetlands. A spacious lawn bridged the gap between a ravine and my sun room, and even though Amy wasn't crazy about the small house, I told her that our son would need outdoor space to play when he was older. You know, throw a baseball around, kick a football, wrestle. He could climb the big old oak tree in the middle of the yard, maybe break an arm to build character.

Plus—plus!—there would only be three of us. Additional habitat would be wasted. These are the things I told Amy to convince her to move into the modest house with me, even though the primary reason, for me, was the trees.

On an ideal morning, I would sit in the sun room and have a coffee. I watched the squirrels playing outside, and listened to the birds chirping their inscrutable communications. On an ideal morning, I would sit there for twenty minutes, becoming relaxed, refreshed, and, if not eager for the rest of the day, at least prepared to tolerate it.

Most mornings were not ideal. Inevitably, I would be torn from my routine by Amy or Todd, requiring one thing or another. Amy needing me to make a sandwich for her because she is running late. Todd needing me to sign a form for a school thing. I would tense at first, but then take a last look at the trees, swaying with the demands of the wind, and accept the interruptions. Being a good husband and father is about sacrifice. That is why most mornings were not ideal.

It was, however, on a rare ideal morning when the tree appeared. February had brought a light coating of snow. I marvelled at the beauty of the morning sun twinkling off of the fresh, fluffy powder. I drank my coffee, infused with a hint of chocolate flavour, and stared at a cardinal singing on a fir tree in the distance.

Then I noticed it. What first grabbed my attention was that it had no snow on it, though I did not deliberate on this point any further, for the strangest thing about the tree was that it had not been there the morning before. I was sure of this, because I at least *attempted* to achieve an ideal morning every single day for the last fourteen years, absorbing the landscape in its entirety, becoming part of it. There was a row of trees before the drop of the ravine, the oak tree in the middle of the yard, and now, this new tree, between the oak and the house.

Its colour also struck me as out of place. Red. More maroon than cardinal red, perhaps, but unusually radiant for a tree in the winter. It was small—two feet tall, maybe—but it did have several branches already. How could a tree that was no more than twenty-four hours old be the size of a toddler?

I called for Amy, and she arrived a minute later. She was still in her underwear, fiddling with an earring as she walked into the sun room. Her thin arms caught the light while she stuck her elbows out, and for a moment I didn't mind having her in the sun room. I was, I reminded myself, very lucky to be a greying middle-aged man with a pretty wife, a house, a young family.

"Do you see that red tree?" I asked her. "I could swear it wasn't there yesterday."

"Nah, Wes, of course it was there yesterday," she said.

"Are you sure?"

She squinted because she couldn't see very well without her glasses. "It was probably under the snow. Why?"

I ignored her question. "So you're not sure. Well,

I'm certain it wasn't there yesterday."

She made a questioning hum, then turned around, still trying to get the earring into her ear. She paused at the door and turned back to me. "Oh, could you write that check for Todd? He needs it for his design and technology class."

"Sure," I said. I bit my lip. She seemed to hardly care about the sudden appearance of a red tree in our yard. As if she hadn't even heard what I said. She always did things like that. I took a breath. It was fine. She had her own things to worry about and, maybe, for people like her, a strange plant was hardly worth a thought.

"K, thanks honey," I heard her say as she walked away.

I sat for a few more minutes, finishing my coffee, then went into the kitchen. Amy had already left for her job at the security company. I was running late myself, but remembered to sign the cheque for Todd's shop teacher, whose name he had left in barely legible scrawl on a Post-it note on the counter. I made a mental note of my own to look up the growth rate of trees when I got to work.

I could still see it through the back door, as if it did not want me out of its sight. It was unmoving, resistant even to the influence of the wind. I did not believe it possible for a tree to spring up in twenty-four hours, but perhaps there were things in this world I still did not understand.

CHAPTER 2

I had almost forgotten about the tree by the time I got to work, but the smell wafting from the office coffee machine triggered my memory. Testing Internet search engines was part of my job, so the office was an ideal environment to test anything that had been on my mind. I sat down with an early version of some Web indexing software and began trying terms. I tried "red tree" first, and several million web pages were listed. I found pictures of trees with "red" in their name, but none were the same shade as my red tree. The red fir—*abies magnifica*—hardly looked red at all, and I wondered where it got that name. Maybe they pulled a name out of a hat to avoid using the scientific name, which sounded like a magic spell from those Harry Potter books that Todd used to read.

The red maple—*acer rubrum*—had brilliant red

leaves, but the trunk was plain brown. The tree in my yard was red right down to the trunk, and being winter, I didn't see any leaves on it.

"RUBRUM! RUBRUM!" I muttered to myself. "REDRUM! You know?" Nobody heard me. The fluorescent lights felt like they were burning my skin.

I tried several terms related to the rate of tree growth. I was surprised at how fast some could grow. The *paulownia tomentosa* could shoot up twelve feet in a year. However, it looked nothing like the tree in my yard, and I found no trees of any kind that could gain several feet over night.

The searching fueled my interest. My desire. I enjoyed mysteries, and this was turning into a real caper, like the kind Columbo would solve. Of course, he'd be interviewing witnesses, not searching the Internet.

I decided to try a different approach. I would find a tree expert, who I would email about the red tree. I searched in an online ecology journal for tree researchers, and picked one, R. Urban, who seemed to have a lot of publications. I tracked down Urban's email address and wrote him a short message, asking if any tree species could grow a few feet tall in a single day. I also mentioned that it was red. Sincerely, Wesley Burnett. I sent the email, realizing that I had not given him much to go on. Screw it, it was worth a try.

I told some co-workers about the tree during lunch,

sitting under different fluorescent lights, among stale air pushed by fans from room to room.

"You probably just didn't see it before," one of them said. "Maybe it was under the snow." I told him that I would have seen it if it were there, and laughed, because I knew it sounded crazy. It was crazy. Right?

CHAPTER 3

The next morning, I fixed myself a bowl of Rice Krispies and some coffee; this time, I went a little nuts and put a pinch of cinnamon on top of the ground coffee, to add a hint of spicy flavour.

I went into my sun room, hoping for an ideal morning. I sat and listened to the birds chirping and the Rice Krispies going snap, crackle, pop.

When my gaze fell on the tree, I felt as if I'd already been looking at it all night. I could swear that it had grown another foot, but I could not be sure without any nearby objects as a point of reference. I also thought that it had more branches than it used to. Something strange about the pattern of the branches was an irritant to my mind, like walking into a room where the furniture had been moved slightly.

I leaned forward. I heard Todd's voice calling me. I ignored it and stared at the tree a moment longer. Todd called again, louder this time, so I stood and stomped into the family room. He sat on the couch, watching some rap video on the television. "What's for lunch?" he asked. I remembered that Amy was in a rush and asked me to make food for Todd.

"Son, you can make your own lunch today," I said.

"Mom said you'd make me one," Todd said, taking his gaze off the television for a moment to glare at me. His eyes were bloodshot and puffy. He was probably up late playing his video games.

"You're perfectly able to make a sandwich. You can start taking better care of yourself," I said.

"Fine," said Todd, looking back at the TV, "I'll skip lunch today."

I considered giving in and preparing something quickly, as I usually did, but maybe a change would teach him something. He'd become complacent, leeching off of us while he soaked in light from television screens and got fat. Maybe a day of hunger would do him good.

I passed Amy on my way upstairs. She mimed a kiss as she blew past me. While I dressed, I heard Todd complaining about his sandwich, her grumbling about me, then the rustle of lunch money coming out of her wallet. She always did things like that.

At work, I got a reply from the tree expert. I clicked on the message excitedly, hoping that he could provide some answers about the mysterious red tree, but I was disappointed:

Wesley,

Trees do not grow that fast, especially not in the winter. I am
certain that you simply did not
notice the tree until it had grown
to the size it is now.

Best Regards,
Robert Urban

Right. I just never noticed a funny-looking red tree in the middle of my own yard. I rubbed my eyes, tired of everybody saying the same thing.

At least he confirmed what I suspected: trees do not grow that fast. Heck, maybe I *was* imagining it. I supposed it was remotely possible that the snow was deep enough that I had simply not noticed the tree until it peeked above the Earth's fluffy winter shell. I put it out of my mind and got back to work, a little disappointed, because I had hoped the mystery would grow, bearing the fruit of something, anything, to occupy my mind other than the tangle of thoughts starting to push up there. *Todd is disappointing. Amy is disappointed. How did you get here?*

CHAPTER 4

I had dismissed the mystery too soon. The red tree had doubled in size less than a week later. I mentioned this to Amy when she interrupted me in the sun room.

"Weird," was her only response, before rushing off to work again. Yeah, weird. At least she acknowledged that I had spoken. It was better than nothing.

That evening, I found time to get a closer look at the tree. I put on my winter coat and boots, plus gloves I hadn't needed in years, since I never spent much time outdoors. I felt the rims of my nostrils harden as soon as I took my first breath of the freezing night air. I trudged across the back yard's deep snow, realizing that this was probably the first time that anyone had put footprints in it all year.

The tree was about four feet tall now. It was a perfect brownish-red pole that split at the top into four thick branches, which split further into smaller branches. Like most other trees at this time of year, there were no leaves.

Its texture was similar to any other deciduous tree, with vertical ridges running along its length. Except, it did not look *rough*, as bark was famous for being. There were no knots, chips, or other imperfections along its length. Maybe all young trees were like that, starting out perfect and only gaining rough edges as life battered them.

I took off my gloves and ran my fingers along its tiniest outer branches. These were smooth, like little plastic straws. I let my fingers follow its contours, slipping along the elbows where smaller branches met bigger ones, then sliding down each of these branches, angling, repeating, until I was caressing the trunk. This, too, was smooth. It felt more like the velvety skin of a house plant than the rough bark of a tree. Its ridges were like tiny folds in a sheet of silk.

Also, I could swear that it was warm.

On a whim, I bent over and smelled the tree. It was sweet, yet nauseating; a combination of licorice and vomit.

I exhaled a cloud of vapour into the cold air, and took a step back to view the thing in its entirety. As before, a sense that something was wrong came over me. It was not just the colour, nor its smooth texture, but something about the overall gestalt of the tree filled me with worrisome awe that made my heart cautiously increase its pace.

A sudden thumping came from above, startling me. I looked toward the house, and realized that it was Todd's music starting up. That damn rap music. A light was on in his upstairs room. He had a friend over, and I wondered what they were doing up there, with the horrible music blasting so loud. They probably couldn't even hear each other talk.

I took one last look at the red tree, then headed inside. This thing was something special—I was sure of that now—and I had renewed hope that this mystery was important, it was solvable, and it belonged only to me.

CHAPTER 5

*T*odd is hiding something.

I came to this realization the next morning, while I sat in my sun room, glaring at my tree, trying to will it to reveal something.

Todd hardly talked to me. When he did talk, he avoided eye contact. When he did make eye contact, his eyes were red and baggy. He had lost weight. He still wasn't thin, but his skin seemed looser, and his chin jiggled when he walked.

Drugs? No; I had the drug talk with him *several* times when he was younger. I even left an anti-drug book from the school board on his pillow, so he could read it over in his own time. I was not one of those parents that stood aside and let their children explore the whims of their chaos-prone teenage minds. Todd didn't do great in school, but I knew he was too smart to alter his mind with chemicals.

14

So, I took a deep sip of coffee, and created stories about what he was up to. The one I stuck with was that he was having girl trouble. A "crush" on a girl at school who wasn't "crushing" back. Or, he was too shy to even talk to her. I had read on the Internet that depression can cause insomnia and weight loss. Todd was probably too sad to sleep or eat, so he stayed up late, listening to his music and playing his video games, until his eyes were raw. I remembered the torture that girls had put *me* through as a teenager, and this story seemed entirely plausible.

I could have talked to him, and maybe it would have helped, but we never really *talked*. We never threw around a baseball, kicked around a football, or wrestled. Sitting him down for a chat would be yet another anomaly in a teenage life full of them. I loved him, but my love was best experienced at a distance.

I turned my attention back to the red tree. It grew overnight. I had committed its expanse to my memory, so I was sure of this. Robert Urban, the tree expert, had said it was impossible for a tree to grow that fast. I needed to prove him wrong. I went through the house and found two meter sticks, some duct tape, and my digital camera. I put the meter stick into the snow beside the tree. It was already taller than a meter, so I taped the second meter stick to the first. Accounting for overlap between them, the tree was 1.2 meters tall from the ground to the highest tiny branches. I set the date stamp to appear in pictures, then snapped some shots of the tree and the scale. I captured it from all angles and distances, getting close, lying in the snow to get a low-angle shot of its perfectly-posed branches. Work it, baby, work it.

I repeated this process several times over the week. On some days, I saw Amy walk into my sun room, probably looking for me to do something for her or Todd. Through the windows, she gave me a confused look, rolled her eyes, then walked away. She never asked what I was doing. This confounded me, because even if she did not notice the tree's strange appearance or rapid growth, surely my considerable interest in it was out of place. I do not know how she could have such an anomaly staring her in the face and not be curious enough to even ask.

Then again, Amy had never been interested in the same things that I was, so unless she needed something, I did my things while she did hers. Shortly after we moved in, I had asked her if she wanted to go for a hike in the forest on the other side of the ravine behind the house. It looked beautiful, and I wanted to see what it had to offer. Amy refused; she saw no enjoyment in walking around in the wilderness gawking at nature. I went on a hike alone, and it was, indeed, a lush forest with much to offer—too much to fully comprehend, especially without another person to bounce ideas off of. I was overwhelmed at the sheer variety of trees— oaks, birches, pines—each subtly different from every other. I drifted through the sea of green and brown, absorbing the spicy smell of pine needles and fresh soil, then came home refreshed. I wish I did it more, but, responsibility.

At the end of the week, I had quantifiable evidence of the red tree's rapid growth. It had grown from 1.2 meters to 1.5 meters in just one week. Its growth rate had slowed since it first appeared, but its change was certainly significant.

One of the guys at work asked if it was just the snow melting because of the warmer weather. Maybe the meter stick was sinking lower and making the tree appear higher in comparison. He was a bright young man, and the idea was a good one, but I told him that I had made sure to push the stick all the way to the ground before each measurement. There was no question about it: the tree was growing faster than any tree had in the history of plantkind.

I uploaded the pictures to my computer. Looking at the tree on the screen, I was again struck with a sense of unease. I must have detected some difference from the Socratic form of a tree that made it less tree-like than a tree should be. I was also struck by its beauty. Close-up shots revealed tiny dew drops reflecting the early-morning light. Other shots emphasized the stark contrast of the maroon bark against the untouched white snow. Impressed by my photography skills, I hit the print button and stashed several photographs in my briefcase.

I also attached a few key pictures to an email and

addressed it to Robert Urban, the tree expert. I explained how I had taken them over just one week —"note the time stamps," I wrote—and had carefully kept the measurement apparatus consistent. I included a close-up of the bark to show him its unique colour and texture. I wrote that I would love to hear what he thought, Sincerely, Wesley Burnett.

That night, as I emptied my briefcase and removed the printouts, I realized what was wrong with the red tree. I had taken one shot from near the house, looking out toward the ravine. Trees of all shapes and sizes filled the background. In front of these stood the giant oak tree that had been there when we moved in. Then, in the foreground of the shot, sat the red tree. My red tree.

I had thought it was not tree-like enough, but I was wrong. Seeing it in direct comparison to the others, the problem—and I am sure this is what was causing me awe and dread whenever I stared at it for too long—was that it was too perfect. The oak tree had a few more branches on one side than the other, like it decided it was more comfortable resting its weight to the right. The branches themselves stuck out at every possible angle. Some were broken, some were thicker than others. My red tree was almost perfectly symmetrical. Each branch flowed from another branch at the same angle. The tiniest branches at the outside edges were nearly all the same length and thickness, as were all the slightly thicker branches they sprung from, this pattern holding all the way down to the four thick branches coming from the main trunk, reaching at right angles to every direction on the compass.

I pinned the picture that best illustrated this impossible symmetry to the wall of my home office. Then I took out the other pictures and pinned them to the wall, too. I stood for a long time, surveying the pictures of my perfect little red tree.

Then I found the imperfection.

It was only visible in some of the more recent pictures. Looking at the trunk of my tree, one side was a perfect vertical edge—a straight line dividing foreground from background. The other side, however, had a slight outward curve to it. It was bulging, just a bit.

My chest filled with ice. What if my tree had some sort of disease—a fungus or something—that would kill it before I could unlock its mystery?

The bulge was something I would have to keep my eye on.

CHAPTER 6

I heard back from the tree expert the next day:

Dear Wesley,

I apologize for my terse response to your first inquiry. From your photos, it appears that you do have a rare species in your yard. In fact, I do not recognize it at all. I suggest that you continue to document its growth, as you have been doing. I would also like to send a student to take a look at your tree and collect samples, if that is all right with you. My number is below, so that we can

```
discuss this further by phone. I
look forward to hearing from you.
In the meantime, I will do some
research to determine what you
have on your hands.
```

His phone number and address were below. He was located at a university just a few hours up the highway. I did not want to make a personal call at work, so I saved the email and tried to concentrate on my duties, but I could not. A new species! Would I get to name it? Silly sounding names would not do for my tree. I'd have to name it after something I cared about. Nothing immediately came to mind.

I found myself searching the Internet for information on trees and the diseases that could kill them. Eutypella canker was a fungus that could destroy a maple if left untreated, and caused a deformity like the warts I used to get on my feet when I spent time outside barefoot. While worrisome, the disease, and indeed all of the diseases that I found information about, were specific to certain species. Since I had no idea what kind of tree mine was, it was impossible to research what could afflict it. I decided to wait and see how the bulge progressed before worrying. I could ask Robert Urban's student about it when he came to take samples.

I put off calling Urban for a week. I was always too busy or too tired, and the phone was not my preferred method of communication. Perhaps I could insist he emailed me back. Every day, I documented the tree's growth with my digital camera and the meter sticks. I had to buy another stick and a metal pole to stabilize the measuring apparatus, because the tree was nearly 2 meters tall by the end of the week.

One morning, after measuring, I was overcome with a sense of terror generated by the tree's unnamed anomalies. I stared until I could identify what jumped out this time—something I should have noticed in the pictures. It was a particularly cold morning, and all the nearby trees had fluffy puffs of snow atop their branches. My tree, however, was bare. I bent close and watched as snowflakes lightly touched down on its branches, then immediately melted into droplets. I took off my gloves and stroked a branch. Now I knew that I wasn't imagining its subtle warmth.

My fingers flitted along its branches, working their way down to its trunk. With my face close, I could smell its sickly-sweet odour. I slid my palm down the trunk, feeling its warmth. I got to the curved side. The bulge was bigger now—a deformity that would surely be noticeable even to an unfamiliar eye. It sloped smoothly down and out from about halfway down the trunk, then abruptly joined the trunk again near the bottom. Like half of a teardrop. The bark around the bulge did not split or strain; the ridges had simply flattened to accommodate the bulge. As if it had been meant to expand all along, accordion-like. My worry for its health was replaced with a more cosmic fear: an intuition that the bulge was a natural part of the tree's lifecycle. Perhaps all trees of this kind grew bulges. If there were any more of this kind.

That night, I woke up suddenly from a peaceful sleep. At first, I had no idea why I was awake. The clock read 3:12 A.M. Then I heard voices, coming from outside. I heard the crunching of snow. My heart thumped, fast and frustratingly loud in my ears.

I laid motionless, not daring to breathe, so I could hear every noise. Had I imagined it? Sweat prickled my brow. I struggled to decide if I should get up and check the window, or ignore the problem, Amy-style, until I drifted back to sleep. Then I heard more crunching, in the unmistakable pattern of footsteps.

I jumped from the bed, flicked on the bedroom light, and raced to the window. At first I saw nothing, but then out of the corner of my eye, movement. A figure stood just outside the range of my sight. All I could make out was a pale orb, connected to the earth by a long, dark body. I thought for a moment that it was my imagination, but then a cloud of vapour puffed from the figure just before it disappeared into the darkness. Someone's breath in the cold air. That couldn't be imagination; my imagination wasn't smart enough to add that detail.

Amy's reflection in the window, sitting up and rubbing her eyes, obscured my view of the yard, and I realized how stupid I was to turn the light on. I ran to flick it off again, but when I'd returned to the window, the figure was gone.

"Honey, what the fuck?" Amy's voice was hoarse.

"I saw someone out there," I said. I could still hear my heart thumping. "I heard voices. Someone is out there."

"Honey, it was probably the neighbours," said Amy.

"No, I saw something! In our yard!"

"We'll worry about it in the morning." She sighed and rolled over.

Typical Amy, putting it off. She always did things like that. I considered calling the police, but there wasn't much to go on. Besides, with my heart racing with fear, excitement, and a bit of anger—and with both of us already awake—my thoughts turned away from the figure outside and onto the one in my bed. I slid under the covers and caressed her breasts from behind, my chest against her naked body.

She breathed heavily, as if she had already fallen asleep, though I knew she hadn't. My fingers slid lower, and she rolled onto her stomach to block them.

I groaned and rolled to the other side of the bed. I didn't sleep for the rest of the night.

CHAPTER 7

I went downstairs feeling like I was hung over, though I had not had a drink in fifteen years. My father, and his father before him, battled alcoholism. Except battled is not the right word; they continually chose to get in the ring with alcoholism, and lost every time. I didn't enjoy being drunk enough to risk continuing the tradition.

Todd came downstairs just after me, also looking like he'd lost a fight in his sleep. I grunted a hello, and he grunted one back. You could say we shared a moment. I prepared four cups of coffee, extra strong, poured it into a large Thermos, and took it to the sun room. This morning was already far from ideal, and the last thing I wanted was to be interrupted.

Of course, interruptions were what I got. Amy burst into the room, running late again and asking me to make Todd's lunch. She didn't mention the night before, which did not surprise me. I was still not entirely sure if the figure in the yard was real, but if there was even a chance, it was something that needed investigation. Discussion, at the very least. As Amy babbled unrelated instructions to me, I stared at the yard and said nothing. She seemed to take this as agreement.

I had a few minutes of peace after she rushed off. Outside, grackles squabbled with sparrows for the best tree branches. Then Todd yelled from the kitchen, something about lunch.

"Get your own damn lunch," I shouted.

There was a moment of silence. Then, "fuck this."

A moment later, a door slammed and I was left in silence.

My head pounded. I felt anger and guilt rolled into one, gnawing away at me like a pair of teeth from a squirrel preparing a nest in my skull.

Then, staring out the windows of the sun room, I spotted footprints. My footprints, of course, were all around my tree, but now a second set led away from the house toward the ravine. I hadn't been that way in a long time. I pictured the figure my groggy eyes had beheld: a white head and an elongated dark body. Now, here was physical evidence that it was no figment of my imagination, and it was certainly not the neighbours.

I needed to photograph the footprints. For the police, so they could identify the intruder by their type of boot, like they did in that CSI show I sometimes found myself unable to stop watching. With photos, they would definitely catch whoever was sneaking around my yard, around my tree.

But I could not find my camera. I could have sworn I'd left it on the dining room table—a table we used for storing junk more than eating on—but it was gone. I searched everywhere it could have possibly been. Gone.

Was it stolen by the figure? Its footprints led from the ravine to my tree, where my footprints were everywhere. From my tree to the house, it could have walked in my prints to hide its own. I could have slept through the noise of the figure breaking into the house, and only noticed it as it fled.

Why was I referring to the figure as "it"? I saw it in my mind's eye again: a round, white orb, with a vague impression of eyes, steaming in the cold. No hair, no hat. I had heard voices, too; there must have been more than one.

I went from room to room, checking for anything out of place. Nothing else appeared to be missing. Why would a person silently break into a house, only to steal a camera before taking off?

What the Hell was it doing near my tree?

Too many questions. Too many mysteries.

I called in sick and bought another camera. I documented my entire yard, careful to take a picture before each step forward transformed the crime scene with my own footprints and filth. I pictured biological material—skin flakes, bacteria, spores—shedding off of me like fairy dust, contaminating the preserved environment.

The sun had come out to erode the figure's footprints, so they only looked like oval indentations in the snow. No way to identify the impression of a boot, or a foot, or a gnarled claw, which did not bode well for the CSI team.

I snapped a picture of the big oak tree, just in case the old thing was hiding any clues. I panned down to take a shot of the base of the tree, then noticed an odd smudge in the snow. I bent down. Dark specks surrounded the base of the oak. I touched the bark, and a strip chipped off. This had never happened before. Under the spot where the bark had fallen off, I could see black lines criss-crossing the smooth underskin of the trunk, like lines of infection spreading from a dirty wound. The old oak appeared to be dying.

My concern turned to my red tree. The oak had a good life, and with time all things must rot, but what if its disease spread? I approached my tree and caressed its trunk. It was as smooth as ever, with no sign of infection. I ran my fingers down its trunk, over the smooth curve of the bulge. I kept my hand there, feeling its warmth.

From where did this concern arise? The oak had been in my yard since we moved in. It was one of the *reasons* for moving in, for Christ's sake. Now it appeared to be sick, and all I could do was worry about this new *thing* that had appeared overnight. I headed back inside, trying to ignore it, but it was visible from every window, unrelenting. *Disease. Rot. Death.*

I found myself back on the Internet, searching for ways to save my tree from the disintegrating world around it.

a week passed. I did not go to work. I told my employers that I felt ill, which was somewhat true. I'd been so dedicated to projects at work that I hadn't taken a sick day in two years, so my manager could not protest very strongly.

Amy kissed my forehead and wished me well before leaving every morning, but she didn't ask what was wrong or offer to help. Todd begged me to let him stay home too. He said that if I could stay home, then he also ought to be able to. It's nice to be a role model to my son.

After a few days off, I let him skip school. Why not? I thought that spending some time with the kid could be good for the family. Bonding time might make me feel better about myself and take my mind off the ... other things. *Disease. Rot. Death.* The words floated through my mind whenever I spotted the tree, framed

30

in one window or another.

However, despite some cursory attempts to talk Todd into watching TV with me, he spent the day in his room. I sent him back to school the next day, even though he was on the verge of tears when he asked to stay home another day, and really was looking unwell.

I spent the afternoons drinking coffee and sitting in the sun room. When I tired of that, I sat on the couch and watched TV. There was nothing interesting on during the day. The talk shows were all troubled families arguing for the audience's entertainment; the news was all doom and gloom because of the earthquakes; and even the "learning" channel had degenerated into conspiracy-minded garbage about mysterious lights in the sky and aliens. So I also got bored with that, and instead, I spent time doing research. I read of diseases that could spread from tree to tree, carried on the backs of worms and insects and other unsophisticated creatures. I got another email from Robert Urban, who I still had not gathered enough time or will to call back:

```
Wesley,


I have not heard from you yet, but
I am afraid that may be my fault,
as I have been rather unavailable.
Some new opportunities have
arisen, adding significant load to
my already busy schedule. Perhaps
```

we can continue our correspondence
later in the year.

Robert Urban

An idea occurred to me. What if the figure in my
back yard that night was not a thief after all, but Urban,
or one of his students? Tired of waiting for me to
contact him, he had searched for my address and come
to study the tree himself. Why would he not tell me
about it? Well, because he wanted to claim the
discovery of the new tree species for himself. Give it his
own name. First, he would have to verify its significance, of course. And after that, well, he'd have to get
the entire tree in order to study it and publish the
results and steal the discovery from me. He'd need to
dig it up and take it with him. This, he could easily do
this in the middle of the day, when nobody was home.

A crazy idea, I knew, but an idea that took root in a
mind made fertile by too much caffeine, and it grew
throughout the week, sprouting tangents and hypothet-
ical horrors that put my tree and my family at risk. I
decided to stay home for a few more days.

I found myself walking back to the sun room hourly,
checking on my tree. It was still growing, and the bulge
grew with it. It now looked stranger than ever, with the
teardrop deformity hanging off one side of otherwise
symmetrical perfection.

One night, I woke with a start. I listened, wondering

if I'd heard whispers, if it was only the rustling of the trees, if it was only in my head, or if it was some combination, all of the above. I heard nothing further. Nevertheless, I jumped from bed and went to the window. Nothing further to see, either.

"Stop movin' around," mumbled Amy.

Instead of returning to bed, I tip-toed downstairs. Something had woken me, and if there was even a chance that scheming graduate students were trying to prod at my tree, I needed to be out there.

I flicked on the light out back, so that I would startle anything that was creeping in the dark. I looked for movement. Nothing. No sign of any figures. No footprints, no pale face, nothing.

I crunched across the lawn, my heart leaping at every shadow at the edge of the light's range. It was freezing, but I took my gloves off so I could feel my tree. It warmed my stiffening fingers. I cupped the tree's bulge in both hands, and then, it moved.

I pulled back. It wasn't much—only a subtle vibration—but with my senses in overdrive, it was enough to shock me.

I bent down and put my ear against the bulge. I could smell the vomit-licorice of it, stronger than before. There was silence for a minute, but then I felt it vibrate again, accompanied by a sound: a quick gurgle. I was immediately transported back to when Amy and I used to cuddle on the couch, watching TV. I would lie with my head on her stomach, and occasionally I would hear gases in her belly push through sphincters in her intestines, making little gurgles, and we would laugh. I would hear the same noises, louder, when her belly bulged with the fetus of Todd. Those were exactly the sounds that my tree had started to make.

I stayed, bent with my ear to the tree and my face away from the house. I heard a few more gurgles. What mysteries this tree had chosen to give me. I closed my eyes, and let a chemical soup of feelings trickle through my mind—confusion, hope, nausea, helplessness, responsibility, duty.

When I opened my eyes, there was a face staring at me from the darkness.

Bulbous eyes picked up the reflection of the light and twinkled in the blackness. As I bolted upright, the glint disappeared and I heard footsteps crunch in the snow, moving right, along the ravine. I bolted into the darkness. The footsteps sped up, and so did I. The snow was deep here in the unmaintained brush and my legs ached immediately. I ran past our yard's side fence and into our neighbour's yard, still hearing movement in front of me.

As my eyes adjusted to the moonlight, I could see the figure's footprints. I aimed my own feet into the indentations, which would surely give me a speed advantage, if I were not already getting winded. I hadn't run in years.

As my eyes further adjusted, I could see the figure ahead. It was a bobbing white orb against the oily black sky. This had to be the same thing that I had seen before. I could just barely make out billowing black below the white head.

A fence lay ahead. This one went all the way around somebody's yard, rather than only along the sides. The ravine dropped sharply behind the yard, leaving only a narrow ledge between the fence and a fall into a freezing stream. Discarded wood and overgrown vines obscured the path. The figure paused for a moment before pushing forward, but in that hesitation I gained ground. I was nearly upon the figure before it disappeared behind a clump of bushes.

Without hesitation, I turned sideways and shimmied along the ledge. Weeds clawed at my feet, and I felt my shins bang against stacks of wood, but I continued on. I reached the clump of bushes, then clawed it aside and stepped over.

A searing pain shot up from my foot.

I looked down, and in the moonlight I could make out a shiny object sticking to the top of my boot. I thought a piece of ice had gotten caught on it, but when I tried to take another step, a slab of wood stuck to the bottom of my boot; it hit my other foot, and I tripped. My face hit a branch on the way down, and I cried out as my face and my foot screamed in simultaneous agony.

I looked up. The figure had stopped at the sound of my cry. It looked back, and I momentarily forgot about my pain. The figure's eyes were too big for its face. My vision had blurred, but I could swear those eyes had no pupils. They were black orbs within a hairless skull. I could not help but think of the drawings of aliens they showed on the daytime television shows.

The figure stayed a moment, motionless, staring at me. There was absolute silence as it eyed me curiously, its black eyes unblinking. It took a step toward me.

Then a light came on nearby, and the figure bolted, quickly fading into the darkness.

A sliver of light poured through the fence, and I got a clear look at my foot. A rusty nail was poking from the top of my boot, fixing my foot to the board that the nail was driven through. My foot had twisted at an uncommon angle, and I suddenly noticed the pain in my ankle as well as in the hole going straight through my foot. Blood dripped from my boot, leaving black-looking spots in the snow. I could feel another trickle of heat down the side of my face. I took another look toward the direction the figure had gone, then began calling for help.

CHAPTER 9

During the hospital stay, Amy stayed by my side. I could tell that she didn't want to be there, and she frequently stepped outside to call colleagues on her cell phone, but she was there. And I appreciated that. I loved her for that.

"I'm sorry I didn't listen to you the other night," she said, shortly after my arrival at the hospital. "I've been ... distracted." Her eyes filled with tears, and she stroked the side of my face with her fingertips. "I'm sorry, honey."

Tears also welled up in my eyes, and I told her that I wished things were different too. That I had also been distracted. I felt a moment of intimacy that I didn't realize I'd missed. Amy kissed my forehead and held me, and, at that moment, all the crap about being angry at her very presence, and all the crap about the tree, and the figure in the yard, seemed distant and unimportant.

Todd came to visit too. I saw genuine concern in his puffy eyes, which was the first time in months that I'd seen him express an emotion other than anger. I hugged him and asked him if anything was wrong, if there was anything he wanted to tell me.

"Dad, I'm not the one with problems right now," he replied, and patted the cast on my foot. It hurt like Hell, but sent me into a fit of hysterical laughter. Todd laughed, too—another thing he hadn't done in a while —and we giggled together.

Some of the best small moments of my life happened in that hospital bed.

I had a monster headache on the day they sent me home. I think it had something to do with coffee. Although Amy brought me some in the hospital, it was not nearly as strong as the stuff I made at home. I'd seen people at the office quit coffee cold turkey, and they spent their mornings in a daze, like zombies with hangovers. I decided that rather than return to my strong coffee, I'd sleep off the headache and gradually cut down on caffeine. Anything that made my head feel like this could not be good for my health. Cold turkey wouldn't work, but I could start by cutting back to watery hospital coffee before switching to decaf.

I'd be on crutches for a while. The rust-crusted nail that punctured my foot not only left an infected hole, but managed to keep my foot still while the rest of my body toppled over. The point between my stationary foot and my falling body happened to be my ankle, now snapped in two places and in constant pain.

Amy had to assist me up the stairs. I took a glance out of the bedroom window before lying down. My tree had not grown much in the days I had spent in the hospital, but the bulge on its side had. It was no longer subtle about its presence. The bulbous deformity stuck out further than the trunk was wide.

I lay down and had a chance to think. The broken ankle aside, my vacation from viewing or contemplating the tree had been pleasant. I'd spent quality time with the family, and anyway, wasn't it unusual to be so obsessed with a tree? Still, thinking about it again did feel familiar. It felt right. I couldn't abandon the tree cold turkey. I remembered that just before spotting the figure, I had heard sounds inside of the tree's bulge.

My head pounded in pain, and an idea came to me: something alive was growing in there. The bulge looked like a pregnant woman's belly, did it not? Also: it was warm to the touch. Animals generate warmth, not plants. Maybe it wasn't really a plant, but some massive stationary animal of undiscovered species and origin. Or—and this idea felt more plausible—perhaps the tree was an animal's cocoon.

The tree was *important*. It could be preparing to give birth; a miracle, according to some humans. Plus, something else was interested in it.

The figure.

A fresh explosion of pain erupted in my head. The figure must have been after my tree. Oh, sure, it had broken into my house and stolen a camera, but could that not have been a clever distraction? An act of camouflage?

When I called the police after my injury, they told me that they would keep an eye on the neighbourhood, but there was nothing more they could do. The figure I had seen was, after all, in the ravine and not technically on my property. My injuries were the result of my own clumsiness, not malice. I couldn't very well tell the police that an unknown entity was trying to steal my weird plant.

I didn't mention Robert Urban. I had no proof. Because it's crazy. *Crazy*. Right? I certainly didn't tell anyone that the figure had abnormally large, unblinking black eyes. *That* was beyond crazy.

The pain in my head intensified, and thoughts bled together. Images of grad students, aliens, and grad students dressed as aliens danced in a circle. And in the center of them, a many-limbed thing, like an enormous red stick insect, about to give birth.

Crazy. I needed this mystery to be over, and it would be over when that bulge burst and let out whatever was inside. As soon as that happened, I could get over this. Cold turkey. Life would go back to resembling that day in the hospital room. Loving my wife and giggling with my kid.

And to return my life from its spindly clutches, the tree would have to survive. Come to term. Shed its pupa. Aliens and sneaky grad students were things that I could not control, but there was one threat to my tree that I could do something about.

Disease. Rot. Death. I could hear the words whispered in the creaking of branches.

A shred of certainty in my confused, pounding head relaxed my nerves, and I finally fell asleep knowing that tomorrow I would be able to take control of this mystery, in some small way. And cut down on coffee, too.

*a*my asked me what the Hell I was doing when I hobbled into the garage and came out with an axe and a shovel. I passed her on my way to the back door, trying to clamp the tools against one of the crutches.

"That oak tree in our yard is diseased," I told her. "I need to chop it down before it … falls down, and damages the … house."

"Honey, you need rest," she said.

"Rest will drive me crazy. It's only my foot. I'm not going to stay in bed all day because of one little hole in one foot."

"So you're going to chop down a ginormous tree with those little rusty tools? While in crutches?"

She had a point. I furrowed my brow, thinking of a comeback.

"Honey, what's wrong?" she asked before I could

reply. "You've been obsessed with yard work. We've barely talked about what happened. Are we okay?"

"Yeah," I said, "yeah, we're fine. I just have to take care of a few things and heal up. I promise I'll be back to my charming self."

She rolled her eyes playfully, but I saw worry flit across her face. "Okay," she said. "Well, a good start would be hiring someone to dig up that tree instead of marching out there on your own like a limpy lumberjack. Let someone else worry about it."

I told her she was right, and kissed her on the forehead before she let me know she would be home late again, then headed off to work. She was late a lot. Something about a new business opportunity at the security company that she had to put time into. Begrudgingly, I made a few calls, and found a landscaping business that would get rid of the tree for a reasonable price. I told them I wanted it completely gone, roots and all. I didn't want the tree's diseased tendrils wrapping their black death around my red tree.

Some large men arrived with large machines, and I pointed them to the oak. First they cut it down with a chainsaw. It was evident that something was wrong, for branches chipped off before the chainsaw got through with them; the vibration alone caused a rain of crumbling twigs.

"Yup, good thing you called us," said one of the men, after hours of cutting away at the diseased thing, "this one was on its way down."

The men drove a vehicle they called an excavator into the yard. They used its scoop to dig under the dead stump, then lift it from the ground. It seemed to pop out of the thawing earth easily, like an old splinter finally plucked from healing skin. Odd; I had expected hundreds of thick roots putting up a fight.

"Strange, eh?" said the large man, "I ain't never seen a tree slide right out. It ain't got roots!" Indeed, the few roots that did poke from the bottom of the stump only reached a few feet before stopping in a dripping wet end. As if they had all melted off.

The men lifted the chunks of tree and stump into a dump truck. There was still a gaping hole in my yard. When I asked one of the men if they were going to fill it back up, he said he'd have to call someone else, that it would cost extra, and it'd take a few days to get the soil in. I told him not to bother. I paid them, then went back to my yard to figure out how I'd fill the crater that now disrupted the landscape.

I stood for several minutes, propped on my crutches, judging how much dirt I'd need. Then I smelled sweet decay. It was like my tree—the licorice-vomit smell—but overwhelming. I moved closer, bent down, and sniffed. I almost produced my own vomit due to the stench. Then, staring at the muck in the hole, I spotted a hint of dark red. The unmistakable colour of my tree.

I eased myself into the crater. I got on my knees, to avoid putting any pressure on my foot. My hands came down on cold mud. The smell was nearly unbearable, so I forced myself to breathe through my mouth. I could almost feel the damp air stinging at my lungs. The reddish spot peeked through the muddy base of the crater. The mud was more than just wet soil—a foul black gel squished up around my fingers as I crawled. I reasoned that it must have been the decayed remains of the tree's roots. The filth that all living things turn into, someday.

I scooped away this gunk around the red spot, revealing more red. There appeared to be something buried just below where the machine had scooped the hole. I clawed away more gunk, tossing it over the lip of the hole, until I had uncovered a portion of it.

It almost resembled another red tree, buried and horizontal. A shaft of the same reddish-brown bark that made up my tree ran from one side of the hole and into the opposite side. There were no ridges on this one, however. I peeked over the edge of the hole where the shaft emerged from the hole's wall and, unsurprisingly, if the shaft continued a few more feet underground, it would connect with my tree.

A root of some kind. That must have been what it was, though all roots I'd seen were spreading, dendritic things. This was a solid tube of bark.

Some of the oak tree's roots wrapped around the tube. Leaning closer, I saw that there was black gunk where the oak's roots had wrapped around my tree's tube. I brushed my finger over one, and the oak's root globbed aside, leaving a smudge of black goo on the tube.

So, this underground root had gone under the oak tree and disintegrated its roots. Maybe spread the disintegration up the oak's capillaries, killing it. I recalled the black lines I had seen under the tree's bark as it chipped off.

That was one mystery solved; one less thing to worry about. Stupid me, I thought the oak tree was the dangerous one.

Now there was a new mystery: what the hell kind of a root was this? It appeared to spread far. The hole was a few feet from my tree, and the root continued on farther still. Did it reach out in other directions? Would I enter my basement one day and find a red tube chewing its way through the wall, like in that movie *Tremors* that they showed on TV all the time? If this was indeed a root, then how did it function without tiny root hairs to wick up nutrients from soil?

Perhaps the tree had read my mind, for this last question answered itself before my eyes. The root had been covered in smudges of black gunk, but as I stared, it appeared to wash itself. The line of gunk that had been left by the snapped oak root was nearly gone. Drops of gunk turned into smaller droplets before disappearing altogether.

The root was absorbing the black stuff. That had to be it: my tree's root disintegrated any plants it came in contact with, turning them black and jellified, then absorbing them.

I put my hand on the root. I felt a faint vibration—the sensation that something was moving in there. I had thought that property was unique to the bulge part of my tree.

Perhaps it even attracted its prey's attention before destroying it.

I suddenly pulled my hand away. I may have—though perhaps it was my racing imagination—felt a sharp burning sensation on my palm. It was probably just the cold. I convinced myself that I was tired of sitting there in the mud and it was time to go warm up and wash myself off. I had just spent a lot of time, money, and sanity trying to save my tree. Surely it would not hurt me.

I glared back at it through the window. My hand sure did tingle.

CHAPTER 11

a second mystery was solved that evening, when I checked my email.

```
_Wesley__,

I apologize for being unavailable.
I have been out of town pursing an
important research problem. I do
need you to call me right away. My
personal cell phone number is
below. I have some rather urgent
information to share with you
regarding your tree. I would like
to meet you in person about this
at your earlier convenience. This
is not something that should be
transmitted over email.
```

```
There is one thing I should tell
you. Do not tamper with the tree.
Do not touch it. DO NOT ATTEMPT TO
CUT IT DOWN OR REMOVE ANY
BRANCHES.

I know this is blunt, but please
believe me when I tell you that
this information should be taken
seriously.

Call me.

Robert Urban
```

I was not entirely surprised by the email's unusual content. I knew the tree was important to me, but the message solidified its significance in the mind of another, and that social validation gave my ideas a fertile context to grow within. I felt a mix of dread and excitement soak through my body. I sat in silence, savouring and hating that feeling as it pushed buds of sweat through my pores.

The figure in my yard probably had nothing to do with Robert Urban. That was clear from the desperate tone of his email. If he had already found out where I lived and sent a lackey to investigate, then he would not be begging me to contact him. One more mystery solved—or at least on its way to being solved. I now knew who the figure was *not,* but that left me to wonder who it *was.*

CHAPTER 12

I refused to call Urban. He had forcefully expressed the importance of reaching him, but that was probably for selfish reasons. He may not have been sneaking around my house, but I was surely correct all along about him wanting the discovery for himself. Of course he told me not to tamper with the tree; he wanted the entirety of the credit for scientific poking and prodding. The ominous tone of his email was more of a *reserved* sign than a *danger* sign. More *CRIME SCENE: DO NOT CROSS* than *WORKERS OVER-HEAD*. It had to be.

I flexed my hand, which was pink where it had touched my tree's root.

The dread/excitement premonition continued through the day. It was amplified when I prepared an entire pot of extra dark coffee, and drank it black, in the course of two hours. During this time, I sat in the sun room, letting the caffeine nourish every neuron in my brain as I stared at the yard and thought deeply. Amy and Todd had already migrated to their daytime habitats, so I was alone in mine, and it was—finally—an ideal morning.

I felt jittery, so I hobbled outside. The snow had receded, and the grass was slick. Thunder muttered in the distance, and I could smell the humidity of an oncoming storm. My red tree's red root still ran through the hole where the oak had been. It was completely free of black goop now, and leaning closer, I determined that the entire hole was devoid of it. The root had soaked it all up.

I went to my tree. I tentatively touched its trunk in the middle of the bulge, half-expecting it to deliver a painful jolt. It did no such thing, and its warmth was, in fact, comforting. I had longed to be rid of this obsession—and wasn't I supposed to cut down on coffee too?—but that was forgotten as I put my face to the bulge, smelling its sweetness, and feeling the faint vibration inside. I balanced there on one foot for several minutes, and three times I heard and felt that gurgling movement inside. It was getting more frequent.

Whatever was living inside the bulge would come out soon. I was sure of it.

I did this a few more times throughout the day, hopping outside to be with my tree between bouts of watching TV and self-medicating with even more caffeine. Forget giving it up. I could do that when this tree business was done. Soon.

Todd came home and said "Hi, dad" when he walked in the door, then lingered behind the couch I was sitting on, looking at the TV, which displayed some ridiculous show about terraforming Mars to make it fit for human habitation. His lingering was unusual, for he usually grunted a "hey" upon arriving home, then went straight upstairs. I turned to him. There was a conflicted expression pulling at his face; also a change from his usual air of numb apathy.

"Is anything wrong, Todd?" I asked. He opened his mouth as if he were about to say something, then stopped. His lips assumed a more controlled position, and he said "No. Nah, I'm fine. You?"

Todd's eyes were red—lined with thousands of tiny branches, as I'm sure my own were. I smirked as I shook my head slightly. A hint of a smile came across Todd's face. We both knew that there was plenty wrong with both of us. The wordless communication of this fact felt like the beginning of a better connection with my son. A bonding that was not perfect, but was ours.

The apple doesn't fall far from the tree, they say.

That evening, after Todd and Amy had gone to bed, I stayed up searching the web. I even considered calling Urban, to hasten the playing out of this mystery, so I opened up the email he had sent me. Then I noticed something that had escaped my attention the first time:

```
_Wesley__,
```

This is how his email had started. At work, I often sent identical messages to many people at the same time. When I did this, I would type out the text in a word processor, and I would leave a blank space, _____, at the top of it. I'd paste this template into my email client, and personalize it by replacing the blank space with a name. I could imagine performing this process hastily and leaving some of the line around the name, forgetting to completely delete it. It would look just like Urban's email. He was in a hurry. And he had sent the same thing to multiple people.

Before I could contemplate this further, there was an aggressive knock on the front door.

I got my crutches and swung my way to the door. I awkwardly opened it, and the breath flew from my lungs when I saw who was there.

The figure had arrived.

The figure was no alien, and he was no grad student either, judging by how he dressed. He was a young man, no older than 20, but with a weathered, pale face. Despite the fact that it was dark outside, he wore oversized oval sunglasses which turned up slightly at the outer edges. His head was shaved bald, and he wore a leather trench coat that went past his knees. It was not entirely surprising that I had mistaken him for an alien.

"Todd home?" the figure—the young man—asked.

"W-what?" I stuttered.

"Todd. We gotta talk."

"Nuh. No. No, you can't talk to Todd now," I said, a hint of indignation seeping into my voice. "He's in bed. What is this about?"

"It's important," said the man, and he smiled a toothy fake grin that revealed small, stained teeth. "Please, mister, sir, just let me tell him something. I know he's awake. His light is still on."

"You were in my yard," I stated. I felt my fingers clench tight around the crutches. This damn kid was the one who was intruding on my property, stomping around my tree. He stole my camera. He put a rusty nail in my foot and a cast on my ankle. All this shit, caused by a punk child friend of Todd's. Not an alien. Not even a mystery. I could figure this kid out in a glance.

"No—I mean, well yeah—but just let me talk to him for a second, man, sir. It's important, so let me in, eh?" The kid was looking past me, looking into my house.

"No. Get off my property, now. I'm not chasing you off again. I'll find out who you are and call the police if you don't get off my fucking porch."

He slid his sunglasses off, so I could see his tiny baby-blue eyes. Leaning close to me, his face inches from mine, his breath smelling like beer and smoke, he dropped the forced politeness: "Ah," he said, "that was you." His beady gaze flicked down to my cast, then back to my face. "How's the leg?"

This fucking kid, with his cocky grin and undersized, soulless eyes. I'd seen that look before. From assholes at the office who thought themselves at the top of their game. They'd call me *big guy* and say things like *you probably just didn't see it before* and flash that toothy grin before swaggering away. Like they owned the place.

Now one of these assholes, a child who thought he was better than me, was invading *my* territory, wanting to come into *my* house and harass *my* son. The same child who had been prancing around *my* tree in the middle of the night.

The kid twitched forward, as if he was going to push into the house. My house.

I lost control of my limbs. My fist tightened around the crutch's grip. I became one with the wooden rod, my arm a weighty branch. It flew in an arc from the ground to the kid's pale little face. The end struck him in the nose, sending a spray of blood down the front of his chest as he exhaled in shock.

As if the wind had caught it, I swung the other crutch, the other branch. I hardly noticed the searing pain in my broken ankle. With a wooden clunk, the crutch collided with the side of his head hard enough to send him tumbling to the ground.

My limbs rained down on him. He raised his flesh-covered arms into my way, his alien sunglasses still in one hand. The crutches ignored them and the sunglasses shattered against the kid's face, cutting at his flesh like that rusty nail had torn through mine.

I landed a few more blows, shattering blood vessels, making him turn black and red. His kicking legs finally found purchase, and he escaped my reach.

I realized I was yelling. I don't know long I had been yelling, what words were coming out of me, or if they were my words at all. I almost lunged at him again, but some shred of sanity held me in place. He whimpered in pain, holding his head. A gash in his eyebrow dripped blood into his eyes.

The kid took hesitation as a chance to back away on his hands and knees, tumbling down the steps of the porch before managing to get to his feet. He looked back, and I could see a glint of his ugly little eyes shining through the streaks of red around them. "You'll fucking pay for this. You and Todd will both pay." His voice was calm, and I shivered despite the fire inside of me. He shambled away, his hand tightly pressed to his bleeding head.

Suddenly, the pain in my ankle rushed back into my consciousness in a terrible wave. I fell to my knees. Todd was at the top of the stairs. Tears streamed down his face. I wondered how much he had seen. Amy arrived a moment later, pushing past Todd and sprinting down the stairs.

"What have you done, Dad?" Todd pleaded, through a rain of tears. "Oh God … Dad, what have you done?"

CHAPTER 13

That night, I dreamed about the day Todd was born.

In reality, it was beautiful. Amy held baby Todd in her arms, and I'd never seen her happier. I have still never seen her happier. Her joy was infectious, and on that day, I barely even regretted the decision to have a kid.

In my dream, however, she was delivering baby Todd in a fire-and-brimstone version of Hell. In the rocky desert landscape, flames shot from fissures in the ground, sending maroon smoke into the blood-red sky. I could hear screaming all around me, and I could see hundreds of other mothers lying on the rocky ground, bellies bulging, legs spread.

I was the only father in Hell, squatting beside Amy. She screamed in agony; sweat poured down her face, making her hair darker, matted against her face in branching strands. Blood seeped from between her legs, and I could hardly bear to look, but there was no doctor around so I'd have to deliver the baby myself.

I could see the crown of a pale head poking out. It was covered in black goo in addition to the blood. When I grabbed and pulled, Todd slowly squeezed out. Except it wasn't Todd. The baby's eyes were too big to be human, and pure black. Where its nose should have been there was only a vaguely triangular hole. Its face was a skull made of flesh.

As I removed it from Amy, at first I thought that it had no umbilical cord. But pulling further still, I saw that it had several, all branching from its feet and ankles. Little roots, covered in blood and black goo, were keeping the alien baby bound to my wife, who had stopped screaming. I put the thing on the ground and backed away. It opened its mouth to reveal tiny, razor sharp teeth, and coughed up oily black liquid.

It raised its feet with surprising strength, and chewed at the umbilical roots sprouting from them. More black goo squirted from the severed roots, dotting its repulsive face. I was soon squatting in a red and black puddle. When the roots were severed, the thing flipped over into a crawling position. It regarded me with animal intelligence in its black eyes. It looked off to the side, then back at me, as if making a decision. Then it scampered past me, faster than any newborn should scamper.

Amy was not moving, and her face had gone pale. I

turned and watched the baby-thing crawl away. Around it, hundreds of other mothers lay on their backs in pools of dark liquid, all of them dead. The things that had killed them all crawled in the same direction, toward a rocky cliff in the distance. The sky was darker red in that direction.

One of the baby-things crawled over a fissure in the earth just as a plume of flame erupted. The thing was incinerated, as if it were made of gasoline. I got some grim satisfaction out of this.

Something emerged at the top of the distant cliff they crawled toward. They say you can't read in dreams, and I find that whenever I try, the words are blurred or I can't quite make them out no matter how much effort I exert. The entity on the cliff was the same way; no matter how much I concentrated, my mind would not let me take it in. My emotions reacted even in the absence of recognition, a consuming dread paralyzing me. A blue glow reached the peripherals of my vision and awareness. I stomped my broken foot, hoping the pain would snap me out of the fearful grip the entity on the cliff held over me, and—

I woke up. Amy had walked into the room and flicked the light on. Red smudges dotted the front of her t-shirt, and for a moment I thought I was still dreaming. Then I realized that she had been cleaning the kid's blood off the front porch.

I opened my mouth to thank her, but before I could speak, she said "Not now. In the morning."

With that, she turned off the light and collapsed into the bed with her back to me, becoming as still as she had been in my dream.

*a*my asked me what got into me. I stared at a smear of blood on her arm as she fidgeted with her hair. Before I could answer her question, she was asking more questions, each louder than the previous, until she was screaming.

"Who was that?"

"Why did you hit him so *hard*?"

"What the Hell has gotten into your head?"

"What are the police going to say? They're probably on the way!"

I told her that we would not be calling the police, and that the kid wouldn't either. A little brawl would be the least of his worries with the law. I tried explaining that this was the kid, one and the same, who was sneaking around the yard. That he was the one I chased, and he was responsible for the hole in my foot. He had broken into our house while we slept and stolen my camera.

Todd breathed in quickly.

I turned to him. He hadn't said anything all morning, but stood at the kitchen counter overlooking the table where Amy and I sat across from each other.

"Todd? You going to do some explaining?" I asked him.

Amy half-stood, probably about to interrupt to say that Todd was not the one that needed to do some explaining, but the harsh glance I gave her must have been enough to quiet her.

"He is—was—a friend of mine," Todd said, his voice hoarse. "His name is Jason. Jay. Sometimes we'd," Todd paused, looking at his mother with eyes unable to focus, on the edge of panic. "We'd skip classes and hang out at his place. A bunch of us. Sometimes I'd go there after school, when I told you guys I was going to Chris's or Dean's."

Amy exhaled in shock, but I had a feeling he wasn't done. "Why did you lie? What did you do with him?" I asked.

"Nothing serious, dad," Todd's voice was shaky, that panicky look in his eyes getting stronger. "I mean, marijuana. Just pot, dad. Nothing serious. But it wasn't even about that."

Amy's face went pale. "Dammit, Todd," she said. "We talked about this. We sat down, right at this table, and I told you about drugs. Were you even listening?"

"Yeah, but, I," Todd sputtered.

"What happened after that?" I asked, interrupting. "Why did you say Jason *was* your friend?"

Amy looked at me as if that was the stupidest thing I could possibly have asked.

"Because I didn't want to to do it any more, dad. It was fun, me and the other guys—Dean was there too—and Jay would bring weed and we'd just chill, watch TV, or play cards, or whatever."

"Then Jay started asking for money. I thought that made sense, yeah, sure, so I gave him some of my allowance. He asked for more, and when we didn't have enough, he'd get in a real bad mood. Once he punched Dean in the gut, and Dean showed me the bruise at school. It was bad. His whole belly turned purple and he got sick."

Amy bounced in her chair, like her feet were already fleeing the room. Always with Amy: fill the room with words, set things in motion, then leave. Like a mushroom bursting to release a cloud of spores before dying.

"Then?" I asked Todd, calm, motionless, demonstrating stability.

"We got Jay money however we could. Dean thought of the idea to tell our parents that we needed money for shop class, and to get them to write the check out to each other and say it was the teacher's name."

I remembered writing that check. Being fooled made anger feel appropriate, but I forced myself to keep it buried.

Todd continued, looking at me as he talked. "It was stupid. We had no money, we were all doing bad in school. It wasn't even that fun with Jay pissed off. It wasn't the weed; I just liked having people to hang around with. I'm not good at making friends, you know that. So I said we should quit with Jay."

I nodded, let him continue. Amy looked restless but stayed silent.

"Then Jay started coming around to our houses at night. He'd throw rocks at our windows to wake us up, like in the, you know, movies, and tell us we owed him. He kept saying he'd, you know, he'd beat us up if we didn't get the money. I know he got into trouble with the drug guys, and needed the money pretty bad. Maybe he needed our company even worse. He doesn't go to school, doesn't see people much. He really liked me. Enough to be creepy. But I couldn't be around him. I just wanted to give him what he asked for and get out of this."

Todd stopped. Amy opened her mouth to talk, but I held up my hand. *Wait.*

"I stole your camera, dad."

It was my turn to be surprised. I was so sure that the figure in the yard, Jay, had been the one who stole it, that I was speechless, an inanimate object unable to process meaning.

Amy broke the silence. "Fuck, Todd! You should have told us! We'd call the police and that idiot would be in jail. Mind you, you'd be spending some time grounded too, for getting us into this mess."

Todd teared up from his mother's words, but it was me he looked at. "I'm sorry, Dad. Once it started I couldn't stop it, and I just wanted things to go back to normal."

I got up and embraced him while he cried. "We'll deal with it, son," I told him. "Nature will run its course, and soon this will be nothing."

"I didn't know what Jay would do if I didn't pay him," he mumbled into my shoulder. "I don't know what he'll do now that you hit him."

Amy was saying something to both of us, but I wasn't paying attention. Neither was Todd. As he cried on my shoulder, I told him that I understood. Because I did. I'd gone through this cycle several times before.

Was I not going through it now? With this tree? Maybe I would have been able to intervene earlier if I wasn't so focused on its mystery. As soon as the bulge burst then it would be solved, I thought, and then it would be time to focus on fixing the family.

Amy became louder.

"Shut up, Amy," I said. I'd never said anything like that to her. But she did it. Her face continued to say something, but her voice stopped.

That was better. We just needed a quiet environment for a few days, so the family could move on with a new stage of life, after dealing with its demons.

CHAPTER 15

The moonlight only hinted at its red colour. My tree was inside my bedroom. It loomed from the corner by the window, branches spreading and scraping against the ceiling. Velvety antlers of a massive entity.

The whole thing swayed slowly, as if pushed by a gentle wind that only it could feel. Its belly hung in front of it, softly gurgling. I never saw so much expression in an inanimate thing before.

"What are you doing here?" I asked.

Its branches creaked as it swayed. When I listened closely, there were words among the creaking, the scritching, and the scratching:

Huuurt.

"No."

Hurtem. Hurtem. Proootectme, said my tree.

"I can't hurt my family. I already hurt them enough with what I did. And I was very cruel to Amy."

My tree's belly gurgled suddenly: *GOOD-GOODGOOD.*

"Maybe you're right."

Its branches tapped out decipherable patterns. *Prooo, tct! Tct! Tct!*

"Protect."

Ysss, hissed its belly.

I closed my eyes, trying to block it out, convince myself it wasn't real. But I could feel its presence there, as strong as if an intruder had entered the room and was standing at the foot of the bed, staring, breathing. When I opened my eyes, the room was empty, but outside the window, I could still hear the creaking of branches.

CHAPTER 16

*A*my loved control. I woke up to a tinkling sound, and found her collecting all of her jewelry from the little metal tree on the dresser that was designed to hang rings, bracelets, and necklaces on.

"So I can lock them in the safe box," she explained when she saw me staring. "These things are worth a lot of money and I don't want them going anywhere. Oh, and can you do me a favour?"

"No," I said.

She continued as if she hadn't heard me. "I'll be late coming home from work again. The new business thing is really taking off, I think—you know, with everybody so uneasy lately. Gotta strike while the iron is hot. So I just need you to call the locksmith and book him in for tonight. Get every locked changed, even the garage one."

"I need you to stop talking," I said. This wasn't shaping up to be an ideal morning, so I would have to create one.

"Excuse me?" she said.

I felt something snap (crackle, pop, creak) inside of me, and every flap of her vocal cords seemed to jab at the inside of my skull. "Just shut up. Close your mouth. *Stop. Talking.*" I stood and my fist clenched.

She looked from my fist to my face. Her nose scrunched up like she was miming the emotion of disgust for the benefit of a child. But she didn't say anything, and that was all I had asked for. As I got dressed and followed her downstairs, we were both silent. Maybe she thought that the silent treatment was something I'd regret soliciting, but the quiet of the morning was music to my ears.

When she left without saying goodbye, only pausing for a moment at the door to stare at me with pleading, tear-filled eyes, maybe then I did feel some regret. But this was good for her, even if she didn't know it. And I needed this. I needed to start shaping this little habitat better for myself, to better manage my ... issues.

I checked my email, but that, too, was far too upsetting to allow into my mental environment, so I shut my computer down.

A bitter calm fell over me, and I was hardly surprised when my first instinct was to put on some coffee and inspect my tree. I filled the coffee filter almost to the top to make it strong. When it wasn't strong enough, I poured black coffee back into the water tank and let it filter through the grinds again. I got the biggest Thermos I owned and poured the thick sludge into it. Cream and sugar were distant memories.

I grabbed a lawn chair from the sun room before hobbling outside. The mornings were getting brighter, and my tree looked absolutely beautiful in the orange-tinged light. The bulge was enormous. Bark that had once been folded into ridges was now smooth all the way around the trunk at the point where the bulge emerged. It again clicked with me that the tree had been designed to expand all along. It was silly to ever think that this natural bulb had been a disease. Indeed, it seemed to be the reason for the tree's very existence. The rest was camouflage.

I was afraid to touch it, because the bulge was so tight that it seemed like it was about to burst. It would not be long at all before it did, and then, finally, I'd know. I'd know what the purpose of the tree was, and why it had sprung into my life so suddenly. I lightly— very lightly—caressed the bulge, and there was no doubt that there was movement inside. In addition to the occasional gurgling, there was a constant vibration that communicated its simmering life.

I even thought I could see the movement. Every once in a while the entire thing seemed to jiggle. As if something inside was getting into a more comfortable position.

I thought back to my email.

Message from rurban@ubnf.ca:
IMPORTANT INFORMATION

Message from urbanrobert@sat-
cast.ca, marked urgent: READ NOW
(Re: tree)

Message from robbyrob@hotmailer.-
com: Wesley, YOU ARE IN DANGER.
PLEASE RESPOND.

The guy was getting desperate. Robby Rob? I would not respond; not now, not when I was so close to discovering the answer to this mystery that was entirely my own. All mine.

I sat beside my tree for at least an hour, maybe two, before going in to warm up and get more coffee before heading out again. The day passed. It got darker, and it got colder. At one point I noticed Todd's bedroom light. I hadn't even heard him come home. There were no lights on in the rest of the house.

My fingers went numb from the increasing cold. I yelled up at Todd's window, trying to get his attention so he could bring me some gloves and a coat. I didn't want to leave the tree now, not when it was so close to the end. I yelled for Todd again, then heard bass thumping out of his window: he had turned his music on. That damn rap music.

Fucking kid. I loved him, but damn that fucking kid.

So I went to look for some warm clothes myself, moving as fast as I could with the crutches, occasionally stepping with my bad foot and sending bursts of pain shooting up my leg. I grabbed my coat and stuffed the Thermos into one if its oversized pockets, then looked for my boots, which I liked to leave out by the front door, but Amy always put them away in the closet. Messing with my environment. As I rummaged for them, Todd came down the stairs.

"Dad? You okay?" he asked.

"Didn't you hear me call for you?" I asked, scowling.

"I didn't."

"I was back in the yard calling you, you must have heard me," I said, as I tossed a pair of boots out from the back of the closet.

"No, Dad, I had the TV and music on."

"Fuck, Todd, you gotta turn that music down." I eased myself down and tied a boot on my good foot.

Todd looked at me, a twitch building in his eye. "Fine, dad. Whatever. Have you seen the news?"

I was in such a hurry that I barely heard him. My tree could burst at any second. After that, it would be over, and I could spend all the time in the world with Todd. "Listen, I'll be outside for the night."

"Right, of course you will. Mom called. She's gone to 'visit her sister,' she said." There was a sarcastic tone in his voice. A tear in his eye welled up but did not fall.

I felt relief at hearing Amy had left. Hurting her had

worked. *Protect*, the tree had said. With her gone, it would be protected from her. More importantly: she'd be protected from me.

"Fine," I said, both sad and proud that Todd, too, could see that the landscape had shifted. That he probably understood what was really going on here better than I did. "It's gonna be fine," I told him, and I believed it was true. His face remained full of all kinds of hurt. "How's your problem?" I asked.

"I'm dealing with it. I told Jay he's not getting any more money, and I ignore his calls and emails. It'll blow over. Just gotta stay strong until it does, right? Like a tree?" He smirked. "How's your problem? It's almost ... you know ... *ready* ... isn't it?"

"Yeah," I said, and smiled. "Yeah. It's happening tonight. Listen, Son, I'm sorry about all this. Tomorrow, we'll sit down and talk about it. Clear the air, make this home liveable for all of us. You and me and your mother."

Todd smiled and nodded, but a tear bulged, burst, then rolled down his cheek.

CHAPTER 17

*A*fter I returned to my tree, Todd's music resumed its thumping, and anger soaked into my consciousness again. I had the crazy idea that maybe the tree was the source of the intrusive thoughts —that it sucked away the peace from my home and replaced it with obsession. Yet this only increased my desire to see it to the end. To witness the final plan of this red tree with its terrible power.

The rate at which the bulge grew was remarkable— though I dared not remark on it out loud, for it looked like the slightest disturbance would cause it to burst prematurely. I longed to stroke the smooth red branches, but my tree was now much taller than me, outgrowing even the measuring apparatus, and the branches reached to the dark sky as if they prayed to an unknowable deity. They were as gorgeous as ever: each branch emerged from its parent branch at a right angle, forming a shape that was the same no matter which angle I looked at it from, its gaze following me like the eyes of the Mona Lisa.

Some of the trees by the ravine had sprouted leaves for the spring, but my tree was unmarred. I couldn't even see nubs where the leaves should have grown from. At this point, it didn't surprise me, or even strike me as odd, that my tree didn't need leaves. It got all the nourishment it needed from its roots.

An hour passed, and then another. Todd's music eventually stopped, at what felt like an hour after his bed time, but I didn't dare check my watch, fearing I'd miss something. The bulge jiggled, and I could hear a gurgling even with my ears several feet away.

Soon.

After another hour, the cold started to get to me again. The cast on my leg was not designed for warmth, so my rigid foot, which often felt hot and itchy, now felt like solid ice. My fingers became numb under my gloves. My thinning hair didn't do much for my head, and my ears felt as if they'd snap like potato chips if I touched them.

I held out for another hour. It pained me to put any distance between my tree and myself, but the bite of the cold was more immediate. I backed away to the sun room. I'd keep an eye on the yard, and as soon as I saw any sign of activity, I could race back outside to witness the … happening.

The warmth was welcome, even though my ears and

fingers hurt like Hell as they thawed. I remembered that the Thermos I had filled up earlier was in my coat pocket, so I popped it open. There was still a bit of thick black coffee in the bottom, and the Thermos had done its job by keeping it warm.

I sat in my spot, watching my tree and sipping my coffee. You could say it was an ideal, albeit early, morning. I knew this was crazy, watching a tree well past midnight, yes *yes* I knew. Half of my mind was aware that the other half had snapped (crackled and popped, too). It didn't matter. All that mattered was watching my tree do its thing, which would relieve me of my duties. At ease, soldier.

My tree's bulge jiggled, now visible even from my considerable distance. It also seemed to throb, growing slightly, then shrinking. Breathing.

What a morning. This was what I lived for. The little moments. Sitting in the warmth, sipping coffee and watching nature. Was it not the reason I moved to this house so many years ago? Before the habitat was corrupted by the weight of *family*.

Despite the strongly caffeinated coffee, the room's warm comfort and the rhythmic throbbing of my tree—ba-*bump*, ba-*bump*, ba-*bump*—overtook me. Staring at it, my head felt heavy.

I closed my eyes for only a moment.

CHAPTER 18

I awoke to crackling, popping, and snapping. My eyes opened and registered only darkness. It was still night—surely I had only fallen asleep for a few minutes—but the yard's light had gone out.

I looked toward my tree, sure that the bulge had popped and I had missed seeing whatever was inside crawl away, confirming that this had all been for nothing. Images of the baby-things from my dream snapped into my head. However, in the moonlight I could just barely make out my tree, with its bulge intact. Thank God. But I could also make out something else. A figure stood beside it.

I hesitated for a moment, unmoving, still half-asleep and not entirely sure I had awoken. As I did so, the figure pulled an object out of his pocket. Orange light illuminated him: a black trench coat, topped with a familiar alien head, marred by bruises and slashes. Jay.

A twinkle to the side caught my eye. Something wet was on the ground. The back light was switched off—he'd walked right into the sun room. He'd been so close. Did he even notice me there, dozing before my tree in the heart of the night?

Something smelled pungent and sweet, like my coffee, like my tree, but … not. I bolted from my chair.

Jay lowered his lighter to the ground.

"My man, Todd. Got your attention now?" he asked, not nearly loud enough for Todd to hear upstairs, and he still hadn't spotted me. Perhaps the words fulfilled some hidden requirement in his private mental environment.

He stepped back, kneeling and using my tree as cover for his vicious project. The flame jumped from his hand to the grass, where it formed a blue tentacle of fire that reached toward the house.

"Old fuckin' man, try to kill me. Try to keep me from my Todd. *He will burn up the chaff with unquenchable fire,*" Jay muttered.

Some of the flammable stuff must have splashed on my tree. As I burst out of the sun room, the flame leapt, and—God, it happened so fast—it spread up the trunk of my tree.

It was hardly surprising now, but it was clear that my tree was not made out of regular wood. It burned as if it were doused in gasoline, though I was quite sure Jay's trail of fuel only led to the house, as the tree was not his target. In seconds, the slithering flames had reached its branches.

Likewise, Jay's cheap trench coat was not made of real leather, and the gasoline-splashed synthetic material went up in flames when a branch dripped fire on him from above. My tree, protecting me.

He spun around, trying to pat out the fire on his own back. Then he saw me, limp-sprinting across the yard. His beady little blue eyes went wide with panic. It almost made me grin. Jay turned and ran away from the house, toward the ravine. The idiot continued patting at his back as he ran.

I stopped. There were more important matters than chasing that fucking kid down. Again. I looked up at Todd's window. There was no light on. He'd managed to sleep through this.

There was a light downstairs, however. The flames had reached the sun room, where patio furniture, insecticides, and leather spray had quickly answered the call of the tentacles of fire.

I fought back panic and took a moment to think. There was an extinguisher in the kitchen pantry. I could get it and put out the fire.

A most horrible question entered my thoughts: Which fire? Todd was upstairs, able-bodied, surely about to wake up and smell the smoke. All the doors were locked except the one in the sun room. With my broken foot, could I get around to another entrance, break in, get to the extinguisher, then fight the fire, in time to help? Or was it already too late for me to play a role?

My tree was only a few meters away. The fire had still not yet slithered around to the bulge. I could reach the garden hose around the side faster than the extinguisher inside the house.

I moved toward the house, my thoughts conflicted. In the crackling of the burning tree, I could hear whispering words: *Sssave. Me. Protect. Me.* I reeled with the overwhelming idea that my tree was exerting supernatural influence over my decision to ignore my son. But the true horror came from the knowledge that it was probably not.

In the end, my tree saved me from making a choice.

As I approached the house, a loud, high-pitched whistling erupted behind me. I turned. The flames had reached around the circumference of my tree. There was a hole in the bulge where the fire had licked it, and vapour billowed from it. It was like a bizarre kettle, whistling and shooting steam.

The sound got louder, more shrill, then suddenly the bulge exploded. Black and red gore flew in every direction. A drop of the stuff hit my cheek, and though it first felt cold, after a moment it burned like acid. I instinctively brushed it away.

My tree had a hole in it. The bottom of the bulge was intact, but the top had exploded. It resembled a spout. The gas billowing from it was like no smoke or steam I had seen: thicker, and neither black nor white but tinged with red.

Black sludge poured out of the hole and onto the ground while the gas rose upward. Then the fire directly above the hole started to go out. As the gas rose higher, each flame it touched was extinguished instantly. A gust of wind blew the gas across the flames, and in a matter of seconds, the tree was no longer ablaze.

My feet seemed to move on their own. I found myself walking to the tree. I heard bones in my bad foot grind as I put my full weight on it, no longer feeling it. I heard my heart pounding, even over the crackling of the fire inside the house behind me.

I had thoughts of something emerging from the gas. Some creature, maybe one of the baby-things from my dream, rising from the steam like in a bad science fiction movie. But as I approached the tree, all that emerged from the gas was more gas. It was all for nothing. Up in smoke. I had been caring for this tree, this thing, saving it from imagined threats—disease, greedy researchers, aliens—and all it turned out to be was a tube full of gas. A tube full of gas that was perfectly capable of taking care of itself.

My tree didn't even need me.

Another gust of wind blew. The gas enveloped my face, and I smelled licorice and cherries and vomit and sulphur all at the same time, and my lungs burned. I coughed. My eyes stung. I felt dizzy.

I took a glance toward Todd's room. Tendrils of smoke seeped from the improperly-sealed windows. When was the last time I checked the smoke alarm? I'd been waiting for the right moment, I suppose.

I fell to my knees. I couldn't breathe. My eyes, my nose, and my throat were under attack. As I lost consciousness, I was sure that I would never wake up, and the thought was not entirely unwelcome.

CHAPTER 19

I could not judge how long it had been since I passed out, but it was still night and I was still lying beside the tree. I could hear crackling behind me; my burning house; possibly, my burning son. My lungs were full of acid. My head was about to burst.

I had to get away. The tree—my tree, my life's work—was killing me. I crawled a few inches away, toward the ravine. Away from my house. I began coughing and couldn't stop. Black splotches appeared then multiplied in my vision, until everything was black again.

I dreamed about Todd and Amy, coffee and happiness. I was in my unspoiled house, cooking dinner for my new wife while she played peek-a-boo with my new son. I cut up onions while I sipped coffee. Amy laughed, Todd laughed. The onion fumes wafted up to my face. My eyes watered, my throat stung, and I could feel cold, wet earth covering my hands and face.

Now I was a few meters away from the tree. I must have crawled some distance as I dreamed. I took a glance back. Gas was still spewing from the tree. The gas seemed to be taking my life, but it had saved the tree's. The tree was, unlike me, able to take action to save itself. It must have been feeding on the oak tree that I'd cut down, making my contribution to its life-cycle a net negative. This hyper-evolved plant could feed itself, deal with its own problems, put out its own fires. It didn't need a father.

Not like Todd did. If he were even alive.

I could only crawl away from the mess I'd made. I hobbled another few feet before collapsing in pain and despair.

The dream returned. I'd finished chopping the onions, so I put them in a frying pan. Todd smiled as Amy peeked out from behind her hands, and I was happy, so happy. When Amy got pregnant I wasn't crazy about the idea of offspring, but this was good, this was right.

Then I noticed that Todd wasn't smiling, but grinning, baring rows of needle-sharp teeth. His black alien eyes scanned Amy, then he pounced at her. At the same time, the frying pan burst into flame, burning my hand. I could smell my flesh sizzling as the heat spread to my eyes.

I awoke. I was far from the house and the tree now, almost at the ravine. The burning smell lingered in my nose, but it was not burning flesh. My head was lying on Jay's coat. The smell was chemical; charred plastic. I continued to crawl, but my eyes and throat still stung. I briefly wondered why—I was now quite far from the house's smoke and the tree's gas.

Through blurred vision I spotted something red beside me. A tube, like the one under the old oak, ran through the bottom of the ravine, which I had tumbled into at some point. My God, the tube was even longer than I had imagined. It continued farther still, entering the other side of the ravine. I crawled, every breath a struggle. My eyes watered so badly that the world was a haze. As I reached the far side of the ravine, I attempted to grab at saplings to pull myself up, but each tree pulled free of the Earth, revealing a dripping black stump where roots should have been.

I could not keep my eyes open. I hobbled up the embankment, blind, thinking only about flight. Each breath felt like inhaling needles. Or needly baby teeth. I reached flat ground, but tripped and landed in something jelly-like; muddy, but not entirely cold. I choked and retched, my body wanting to vomit, but I argued with it. We could not afford any time taken away from breathing. Nevertheless, the vomit won the argument.

CHAPTER 20

*M*orning light seeped through my eyelids. My eyes felt better after being forced to rest, but I was already coughing when I woke up. I lay on my side, and could feel something wet running down my cheek: probably vomit, maybe blood. I opened my eyes, and they started to sting again. The ground was black. Even though I could see my breath in the cold, my cheek in the earth felt warm. The sickly-sweet smell of the red tree was strong in my nose.

I forced myself to sit up.

The forest on the other side of the ravine had changed. What used to be a sea of green and brown was now red and black. The tree in my yard was not unique after all, for there was an entire forest of them in front of me.

The beautiful variety of vegetation that had made up the forest—riotous flowers, and bushes, and gnarly oaks, birches, and pines—was now indistinguishable, as it was devoid of leaves and blackened. The trees oozed the dark goo from their trunks, gobs of it spilling from holes and gouges, feeding the underground network of red tubes that connected every red newcomer.

The red trees were identical, right down to the irritating symmetrical pattern of their branches, and the bulges in their trunks. Some had already burst and were spewing red gas into the air. A crimson haze obstructed distant forest.

My eyes burned as I scanned the landscape, but I kept them open, trying to take this in. Still trying to understand.

I attempted to get up, but slipped in the muck. My hand hit something solid, rubbery. A shoe. My gaze crept up the leg it was attached to, and fell on Jay, lying sideways against one of the gas-spewing red trees. He no longer bore the pale alien face that played tricks with my mind in the dark. Where his cheek touched the tree, skin became jelly. His skull seemed to merge with the trunk. Black splotches covered the rest of his head. The dark liquid oozed from his mouth, and from the wound on his forehead where I'd bashed him.

The tree must have burst in his face just as he got near it. Perhaps it had burst *because* he got near it.

I spun around to retch. When I finished, I looked up and could make out flashing lights at my house on the other side of the ravine. Fire trucks, and probably police. I could hear sirens, too, but they were not coming from my house. They seemed to surround me, as if every ambulance in the city were active. In the distance, I could see clouds billowing up across the city. In every direction I turned, deep red blossoms dotted the horizon, puffy at the top like ghostly trees born of trees.

I tried to imagine where Amy could be, but I could only picture her with her back turned to me, as pale and still as she was when she slept.

I could not understand this. The puzzle was too complex. The mystery was all I had left, but I no longer relished even the thought of solving it. How did I get here? If I had let Robert Urban see the tree, maybe this could have been prevented. Maybe he could have figured out where these things came from, or who put them there. Maybe these red trees, with their poison gas, could have been stopped from bursting. I ignored his warnings. Now it was not only my family destroyed, but anyone near the clouds now drifting throughout the city. Maybe throughout the world.

As I hobbled forward, coughing, there was a wet pop beside me and I felt a splash on the side of my head. A nearby tree's bulge had just burst. The gas spewed into my face, filling my lungs.

Finally, I stopped coughing, as my chest refused to expand or contract. The bulge in the tree puckered in on itself, closing the new orifice, as if it had made an error in bursting on me. As if it recognized me. But I'd already gotten too much of it. I fell onto my back as I clawed at my throat, suffocating.

The last thing I saw—and I pray that this was only a dying hallucination—was a shadow, kilometers away, but large enough to tower over the trees even from my vantage point in the mud. The ground rumbled beneath me. A pair of throbbing blue lights pierced the red haze and reached my consciousness—headlights? Eyes? It shifted, the very Earth creaking under its weight, and although my eyes were able to take in its shape more clearly, my mind would not allow it. Like the entity on the cliff in my dream, it was present but unknowable, inaccessible to human understanding.

Most of my mysteries were solved before I left the Earth, but isn't it always the case that more take their place?

CHAPTER 21

*A*s I drifted away with that sick smell in my nose, I was happy to realize that my last thoughts were of family. Not a dream this time, but a memory, from when Amy was eight months pregnant. We'd just bought the house. A television show about terraforming blared in the background. We stood in the sun room together, holding hands, looking over the landscape of our new yard.

"It's beautiful." I said.

"Isn't it?" replied Amy. "He will really love it too." She smiled, rubbing her oversized belly. Then, seeing in my face that I still wasn't entirely comfortable, she added: "Oh, honey, it will be fine. I think you'll love having something to take care of."

I beamed. Something about what Amy said had clicked.

"It will be a whole new world for you," she added.

NEXT: THREE INCIDENTS AT FOSTER MANOR

P.T. Phronk's next novel, *Three Incidents at Foster Manor*, continues to explore the mysteries raised in The Arborist. Wes's story is over, but his wife Amy continues to live and struggle in a world that has been changed forever.

While it is a standalone mystery, readers of The

Arborist will gain a richer understanding of *Three Incidents'* characters and setting in its shared world.

Blurb time:

An old mansion. An apocalyptic storm. Whispering voices in the air. She was right to fear the worst-case scenario.

Amy Burnett has been buried in her work as a security expert. She likes it that way—her dark past can't invade her thoughts as long as she stays holed up in her office. So why the heck has she ended up at a gothic mansion's doorstep in the middle of the night?

It's because Craig Foster summoned her there. Amy's company built the sealed chamber in his basement, for any worrisome worst-case scenario, but now the safe room has presented a scenario of its own: Craig's daughter is trapped inside.

It should be a quick fix. After all, what's the worst thing that can happen when a stranger arrives at a remote mansion on a stormy night? An impossible mystery? A haunting? A visit from the lurking strangers in the woods? Surely not all three—that would require extraordinarily bad luck.

Unfortunately, Amy's been short on luck lately.

Three Incidents at Foster Manor will keep you guessing until the end with a twist-filled, fast-paced, genre-blending mix of mystery, ghost story, thriller, and cosmic horror that will chill you to the core.

Get Three Incidents at Foster Manor wherever you buy books, or at Forest City Pulp's web site.

If you liked this book, there are **two quick things** you can do to help me make more like it:

- Leave an honest review wherever you got this. Even if it's two sentences, it *really* helps other people find the book.
- Subscribe for my news and giveaways (click on the link, or go here: http://eepurl.com/WZPvD). I'm working on a semi-sequel to The Arborist, so I'll let you know when that's out, or when other Forest City Pulp books are on sale. No spam or bullshit.

Forest City Pulp publishes provocative fiction by provocative writers. It was founded in 2012 to take full advantage of the digital reality of publishing, and is designed to evolve as quickly as technology does. Visit www.ForestCityPulp.com for more information, and send us an electronic communication if you would like to get involved.

ABOUT THE AUTHOR

P.T. Phronk writes about things that don't exist, things that might exist, and things that shouldn't exist. In other words, he writes fantasy, science fiction, and horror.

He received a PhD in psychology after writing a dissertation about why people like frightening films. So he literally wrote the book on horror, and continues to tinker with dark creations by cover of night, while by day, he writes about the mysteries of the human psyche as a brain scientist.

ACKNOWLEDGMENTS

Thanks to:

- My family.
- Ronny, for editing.
- A bunch of people at Kboards, for advice.
- That weird tree I spotted out of the corner of my eye on the bus, and never saw again.

PREVIEW: STARS AND OTHER MONSTERS

Here are the first three chapters of P.T. Phronk's debut novel, Stars and Other Monsters. If you like what you see, you can get the whole thing wherever you buy books or at forestcitypulp.com. The first sequel, Of Moons and Monsters, is also available now.

MEET-CUTE

*W*hen the strange woman ruined Stan Lightfoot's life, he was not minding his own business.

It was, in fact, David Letterman's business he was minding. Pictures of the talk show host still engaged in an illicit affair could sell to tabloids for tens of thousands of dollars. Stan grinned at his trusty dog, Bloodhound, wagging her tail in the passenger seat, then turned on his camera.

He was oh so close to getting that picture; Letterman was right there. Stan knew he was in the right place because Bloody had barked when they drove past the row of novelty shops and antique dealers, all peeling paint on paneling, connected by a sagging porch.

"You're a good girl, Bloody" said Stan. Bloody looked at him and sighed through her nose, frowning.

Stan broke off a chunk of his McDonald's hamburger. The dog flipped it into her mouth, swallowed it in one bite, then leered expectantly at Stan.

"You'll get more when we get our picture," said Stan as he scratched the scraggly gray hairs on her head.

Letterman leaned out of the doorway of a gift shop. If Stan hadn't been expecting him, the talk show host would have been unrecognizable. He wore a trench coat with the collar popped to cover most of his face. The rest was obscured by a brimmed hat and tragically unfashionable sunglasses. He held the door for a younger woman, who was also obscured by sunglasses, but most definitely the woman whom Letterman had supposedly ended his affair with.

Bloody put her paws on the window of the car, panting as she stared at the couple.

"Down girl! You want them to see us? Jackass."

The dog grumbled before getting down.

"C'mon. Give her a kiss," muttered Stan as he zoomed in with his camera. The couple disappointed him by shuffling to the next store, one behind the other, as if they didn't even know each other.

Two larger-than-life-sized cigar store Indians—feathers and all—guarded the entrance to the antique store. A bit culturally insensitive, but what else could be expected from this no-name shit-hole stretch of highway? Letterman bowed before the Indians, each in turn, flashing his trademark gap-toothed grin. With a smile like that, the biggest sunglasses in the world couldn't hide his identity.

Behind him, his mistress giggled. Stan snapped pictures, but a smile wasn't enough. He needed something dramatic, something scandalous. Come on, a peck on the cheek. He'd even settle for wiping an eyelash from the corner of his eye, or adjusting the hat on his head.

They disappeared into the store. Stan sighed and rubbed his temples. Bloody leaned over the gear shift and licked his hand.

"Thanks girl," said Stan.

Bloody licked his hand again, then stared at him with a serious expression.

"Oh Christ, you just want more food." Stan reached into the McDonald's bag on the floor to toss his dog a cold French fry.

He zoomed in on the store window. He could make out roughly human forms, but through the tinted car windows and the gloom of the store, pictures came out dim. Stan groaned.

The way the couple laughed and smiled at each other, there was no doubt they were still fucking. Stan didn't even know he'd find them together when he started following Bloody's directions to New Hampshire. He figured he'd catch old gap-tooth on a miserable 24-hour bender, wearing sweat-pants and stuffing himself with Cheetos.

And that would have been great. Maybe five, ten

thousand bucks to Star or TMZ. But when Stan caught Letterman with his not-wife, who he'd been accused of boning, it had been one of the happiest moments of Stan's life.

Just the pictures of them together would net five times more than a drunken solo shot. Ah, but one shot of unambiguous intimacy, selling it as an exclusive to some major gossip rag, that'd get him the mother lode. He could ditch this paparazzi bullshit. Buy a nice house with a pool, then sit beside it all day feeding Bloody all the fries she desired. Maybe he could even help his poor mother out.

Inside the antique shop, Letterman took off his sunglasses. Perfect, except Stan's camera still couldn't penetrate the murk of the shop. He briefly considered going inside, but Dave wasn't a stranger to stalkers. He probably had an evacuation procedure planned.

Letterman unsheathed an antique sword and held it pointed at the woman's chest, his face contorted in mock menace. His lips moved, sending the woman into fits of laugher.

"Wish I could hear what they're saying. I bet he just said something really funny, better than the stuff on his show," Stan said. "I need one of those audio satellite dish things. The ones that the FBI uses to spy on people from across the street."

Bloody glanced back at him, snorted, then returned to watching the window.

"You think those are even real? Or is that just in

movies? Bah, you don't believe me, but I bet they exist. Remind me to get one, huh?"

The couple looked happy. Maybe it was for the best that old Dave ditched his wife to be with her. It was a shame they had to be so secretive. The thought crossed Stan's mind without a hint of irony before a pang of guilt hit him. He pushed it deep down, inhaling as he raised his camera.

The shopkeeper wrapped something in tissue paper. Letterman grabbed the package, paid, then headed for the door. Stan slouched and held the camera ready. Bloody slobbered on the seat.

As they emerged, Letterman's pinky finger wrapped around his mistress's.

"Not bad, not bad," muttered Stan. "C'mon, give me more. Work it, Davey, work it."

Letterman grinned at his mistress. She smiled back.

Stan exhaled, steadying the camera.

There was a sound behind Stan—a screech—but he ignored it while he snapped off picture after picture.

"This is it. Oh my God, this is it," he muttered. Hand in hand, Letterman's head lowered while his mistress arched her back and rose on her tippy toes. The golden morning light around them, fall leaves blowing past the rustic porch, it was like a scene from a romantic comedy. If paparazzi were rightly treated as artists, this photo would win awards.

Their lips touched and Stan's finger squeezed the button. Just before that ecstatic click, his head jerked sideways, knocking his glasses from his face. A thunderous crunch shook the car. Bloody let out a yelp as she tumbled to the floor.

Stan's car had been nudged from the shoulder into the middle of the highway; by what, he didn't see. Stan whipped his head upright. A Mack truck was bearing down on him. He fumbled for the keys in the ignition, turned them. As he waited what felt like an eternity for the ignition to catch, he heard a second crunch, then a third, then a clamor of splintering wood.

The truck loomed over him, brakes screeching.

His car rumbled to life and he floored the gas just in time to avoid being obliterated. He pulled to the safety of the road shoulder before reaching for his dog.

"Bloodhound! Oh girl, are you okay?" He lifted his dog from the floor onto the passenger seat, patting her down. Bloody was glassy-eyed, but could stand. She shook herself off as if she'd just gotten out of a bath, gave Stan's hand a reassuring lick, then propped herself up on the windowsill to get a look at the commotion at the antique shop.

It hurt to turn his head, but when he did, all Stan saw was a cloud of dust and smoke.

"Stay," he said, but Bloody leapt out the door as soon as Stan opened it.

A figure emerged from the cloud. She wore sunglasses not unlike Letterman's, a long coat, and a wide-brimmed hat. As the dust swirled away from her, Stan saw that the hat had a flowery pattern, and the coat was purple. Above that, an unwrinkled face; she was thirty-something, not much older than Stan.

Behind the woman, a VW Beetle had lodged itself into the porch in front of the antique shop. Bloody hurdled into the smoke and fire. "No girl! No!" screamed Stan. He turned to the woman. "Are you okay? Were you driving that car?"

"Must've hit a slippery spot," she mumbled. She was hugging herself, wrapped up in the purple coat as if it was freezing outside, though it wasn't. Her face was red in the few spots visible between the coat, the hat, and the sunglasses.

"Ma'm, are you all right? Did you get burned?"

"Oh honey, don't you worry about me. Just run along now, I'll handle it fine." She brushed herself off and poked at the arm of her coat, where there was a tear surrounded in dark tacky blood.

"I'll call an ambulance," said Stan. "What happened to the people who were standing on the porch here?" There was no sign of Letterman or his mistress. The porch where they had been standing was now largely taken up by the VW Beetle convertible, flipped on its back, wheels still spinning. Splintered beams of wood poked up all around it. Smoke billowed everywhere.

"People? Ah, nope, didn't see any people there." The woman turned to enter the antique shop. "Thank you, young man, for your assistance. You can get along now. Okay, sweetie?"

Bloody trotted from the other side of the car. Stan's

stifled a gasp. The dog violently shook the object in her mouth back and forth. Little tufts of curly gray hair flew off and fluttered away in the wind. Stan's dog had found Letterman's hat, soaked in blood and covered in fleshy hunks of talk show host.

CAREER MOVE

*B*loodhound was not actually a bloodhound. Stan could never figure out what exactly the little bugger was, but at a pudgy eleven pounds, with grayish-brown fur, the bulbous eyes of a pug and the frowny underbite of a shih-tzu, she certainly wasn't a bloodhound. The name came from her gift.

Articles of clothing are what you want. For a B-list celebrity, maybe even low A-list, you can get a signed T-shirt off eBay for twenty or thirty bucks. Clothing traps the skin oils, or the little hairs, or whatever it was that Bloody sniffed to start tracking the owner down.

Presently, Bloody was taking the celebrity clothing thing a little too seriously. She held onto Letterman's hat, growling, as Stan tugged at it.

"No! Bad girl! Leave it!" he said. Finally, Bloody let go. A clump of hair attached to a jiggly strip of flesh rolled off the brim and hit the odd woman's foot. She was wearing slippers.

The woman stared at Letterman's hat, her head motionless, as if she were daydreaming. She caressed her lips with her tongue.

Stan tossed the hat to the ground beside the overturned car. He held up his hand sternly to keep Bloody from running after it again. The dog was really earning her name today.

"Hey, lady!" said Stan. Her head turned slightly. "We gotta find those people, okay? They might be trapped under your car."

"Was it your ride I nicked before I flipped on over here? I'm terribly sorry about that," said the odd woman.

Stan groaned. She must've been in shock. He started to run around to the other side of the car, but then the odd woman was in front of him. She lowered her sunglasses, revealing eyes the color of ice, striking in contrast with her red skin.

"Honey, you don't want to be involved with this, do ya? More trouble than it's worth, I'd bet you."

She had a point. People from the nearby shops were coming out to see what happened. The shopkeeper from the antique store was behind the cracked window, peeking from behind the counter. Sirens whined in the distance.

The smoke started to clear. Stan glanced down.

Lying on the ground, poking from behind the smashed car, was an unmoving, liver-spotted hand.

Unconsciously, he touched the camera still strapped around his neck. From deep in his mind, that Elton John song, Candle in the Wind, began playing in his head. The woman was right. He didn't need that sort of trouble. A beloved celebrity, killed while being stalked by a professional paparazzo? He had nothing to do with it, but he'd never be able to find work again if anyone found out he was there.

"Okay," he said, his lips shaking. "You, uh, you can handle it? Good ... good luck?"

He backed away from the wreckage. Bloody stared at the odd woman with narrowed eyes for a long while before joining Stan again.

Stan studied the details; they told the story of what happened. The parking lot was pockmarked with two shallow pits surrounded by broken asphalt, where the woman's Beetle had bounced twice before bowling into the couple on the porch. A little pile of broken red plastic sat on the shoulder of the highway; the remains of Stan's tail light. He gathered up as much as he could, stuffing the bits into his pockets. The less evidence the better.

On the road, skid marks started at the junction between the highway and a cross road, then formed a curved line to where Stan's car had been, nicking it before hitting the curb sideways, flipping into the parking lot. Stan took in the details. They could be important later.

Rubbing his neck, he stumbled to his car. Bloody hopped to the passenger side. Stan gripped the steering wheel, his knuckles white.

He considered going back to see if he could help. Bloody let out a sharp bark. She stamped her paws, alternating left then right. Let's go.

"Fine, fine, I'm going."

An ambulance sped past him, lights flashing, followed shortly by a duo of police cars. Stan scratched his face, inconspicuously obscuring it at the same time.

He drove and drove, his heart forgetting to beat every time he spotted a cop. He stopped only once at a greasy roadside diner, where Bloody barked until Stan fed her an entire bacon double cheeseburger. A few hours later, he was back in New York City.

He mumbled a greeting to his old neighbor, Mrs. Olson, on the way in, then slammed his apartment door. He stood with his back to the door, eyes closed, breathing heavily, for a very long time. What was the car's license plate? What color were the woman's eyes? Dammit, he couldn't remember the plate number; what if that detail was important? Her eyes though, her eyes were blue. Icy blue.

He opened his eyes. Bloody was on the bed, snoring.

He collapsed on the tattered couch in the middle of

the apartment. The CRT television flickered to life with a labored boing.

Surely the news of Letterman's death would be all over the networks. With the recent scandal, he was already near the top of the celebrity gossip list, and for the gossip shows, the timing of his death couldn't be better. Especially when his mistress had been by his side.

Was she dead too?

When Michael Jackson croaked, five minutes wouldn't go by without his name flashing across the TV. Stan wondered who had taken the last picture of Jackson alive, and which tropical paradise he was living in now.

Would he even be able to sell his pictures? Or would it dump too much suspicion on him? Maybe he should have just stayed at the scene and cooperated as a witness. Ah, but then the pictures would be confiscated as evidence, so he still couldn't sell them, and his career would still be in the shitter.

What a damn mess.

The television image faded into view. It was already tuned to CNN. Stan mashed the volume up button.

He gasped when he saw what was on. Bloody perked up her ears.

There, on the television, was some bullshit story about the pros and cons of the H1N1 flu vaccine. No celebrity "expert" blabbing about Letterman. No live helicopter shot of the ambulance carrying the body.

Nothing on the ticker about the odd woman who'd bowled into him.

He flipped from channel to channel. Nope, nada, nothing. Somehow, the world hadn't found out that David Letterman was dead.

CONTRIVED ENCOUNTER

"*M*aybe it wasn't as bad as it looked," muttered Stan. He sat on his couch, knees to his chest. It had been a week since the Letterman incident.

Bloody lay on her side beside the couch, her belly flab spilling out in front of her. She rolled her bulging eyes.

"Don't you give me sass!" Stan pointed a shaking finger at the dog. "All we saw was the hat. Could've been a flesh wound." He pushed his glasses up on his face. "Even a minor cut on the head can bleed profusely. Or. Or! Or it was the girlfriend that was bleeding."

Bloodhound rolled onto her back, her little legs wiggling in the air in an effort to flip the rest of her pudgy body over to turn away from Stan.

"Okay, fine, I know, we've been over this." He

touched his finger to his upper lip, stubbly from days of avoided shaving. "Okay, what if. What if!" He paused, staring glassy-eyed at the television screen. "I got nothing."

He jumped and shouted, "ahhh!" Bloody flipped onto her feet, her floppy ears perking up. "It's on!"

After a flyby of the Statue of Liberty and a zoom through an animated New York skyline came the announcement of the guests, a lame joke, then the familiar Daaaviiid Lettermaaan. The band's trumpets squealed.

Stan leaned forward on his couch. Bloody rolled over again. She hated Letterman; whenever Stan got home in time to put the show on, Bloody would either stomp out of the room or make a point of snoring loudly. She whined when Stan came up with the idea to stalk the talk show host for a while. Maybe he should've listened to his dog.

Letterman appeared on the glossy stage, the simulated skyline of New York behind him. He looked healthy. Not a scar on him.

"Thank you," said Letterman. He shuffled awkwardly on the stage, made a funny face. The band sounded an orchestra hit, and the audience laughed. "Welcome to the program, ladies and gentleman. I know we've got some out-of-towners here. Don't know if you're aware, that's it's been raining a lot in New York City. Raining a lot in the whole North-East. They're talking about rain tonight; could get some of that high wind, flash flooding. And you know what that means. You folks could be sleeping over."

"Yeah," muttered Paul Shaffer. The audience howled with laughter.

Stan bolted from the couch, then pulled a curtain aside. The sidewalks were deserted, save for a couple entering the pub across the street. Its neon lights flickered, reflecting off of nothing; the street was as dry as a bone celebrating a year on the wagon.

"It isn't raining! What the crap, Bloody."

Letterman was now monologuing about Al Franken getting sworn in as a senator in Minnesota. That happened months ago!

"This episode is from months ago!" Stan collapsed onto the couch. He picked up a beer bottle from the floor and took a swig. "It's a damn re-run again, Bloody! He was supposed to be back this week. Said so right on the CBS web site."

Stan rubbed his temples. Bloody sighed, then trotted over to Stan and rested her head on the couch. Stan turned to her. "What should we do, girl? Call someone? The police? CBS?"

Bloody moved her shoulders up and down.

Stan patted her head. "You're a good girl, you know that?"

The dog darted her eyes toward the kitchen.

"You just ate."

She snorted.

Both of them jumped when the phone rang. Stan sat

up. "I'm not answering it. I just—I just can't deal right now, you know?"

It rang six times before it stopped.

Stan lay back down, ready to pass out for the night.

The phone rang again. He rolled over and pressed a cushion to his ear. Again, six rings, then silence.

"Persistent buggers," he muttered.

It rang again. "Aaargh!" he shouted. The shrill cry of the old rotary phone seemed to pierce into his brain. He bolted upright, making to tear the chord right from the wall, but after six rings, it stopped. He hovered over the receiver, ready to toss it across the room the instant it made a peep.

Nothing. Blissful silence. Only the usual din of sirens way off in the distance. Stan prayed that they didn't draw closer.

He wrenched the blanket on the couch out from under his butt, shook off some pizza crumbs—Bloody immediately licked them up—then swaddled himself in it and lay down. When Bloody had found every last crumb, she jumped on the couch too and took advantage of the warmth of Stan's feet.

There was a sharp rap at the door.

Stan groaned. He sat up, nostrils flared. Bloody bounded to the door and sat staring at it, a low growl on her breath.

Holding his face up to the peeling-painted door, Stan glared through the peephole. It was her. The odd woman who had killed David Letterman. She wore the same flower pattern hat from when Stan last saw her, and a matching flowery dress. When Stan spotted her through the peephole, she leaned forward to hold her icy blue eye up to the other side.

He jumped back. "Ah! It's her! That freak woman!" he said, a little too loudly.

Bloody raised one eyebrow.

"Dammit, you're right," whispered Stan. "Now she knows we're here. What do we do?"

Bloody trotted to a spot beside the door. She crouched, then nodded her head, as if to say, go for it, I'm ready for trouble.

Stan sighed. He ran his fingers through his tangled hair, pushed his glasses up, then opened the door a crack. The chain kept it from swinging open further.

"What do you want?" he asked. He felt Bloody's breath, hot and fast, against his ankle.

Her face was still pressed up against the door. Those eyes flicked sideways to meet his. "Hey Stan," she said.

"How do you know my name?"

"Oh sweetie, I know a lot of things. Can I come in for a sec?"

"No you cannot come in for a sec." Stan frowned and held his face to the opening. He made sure none of his neighbors were in the hallway. "How did you know where I live?"

"I got your license plate in our little mix-up. You see dear, I just need you to sign a couple of papers. For insurance purposes. I'm not very fond of this legal mumbo jumbo myself, but the investigators found your car's paint smeared on my poor car's bumper, so I just had to tell them you were there. I was kind, you see, I told them that you handed me your business card before you left but I lost it. They say we can clear all this up with a few signatures. I tried to telephone before I came over, but there was no answer."

Questions flooded into Stan's head. Chief among them: where was David Letterman? Second: could this situation get him laid? He glanced back in his apartment, all empty beer bottles and mouldy pizza boxes.

"There's a bar across the street. We can talk there. Let me get my coat."

He closed the door. Bloody tilted her head sideways, frowning.

"It's all right, girl. I'll get some answers and clear this whole mess up," he whispered.

The dog sighed.

"Won't be long. Be good," he said.

Under the flickering blueish light in the hallway, Stan got a good look at the woman. Her skin was pale, perfect except for some red patches on her cheeks. She was not much older than he was—maybe thirty two, thirty three—which made her odd fashion choices and odd manner of speaking even odder. Frizzy auburn hair tumbled over the puffy shoulders of the flowery dress that hung off her slim figure. It was either straight out of the seventies or stolen from her grandmother's closet.

As they crossed the street, Stan asked: "Where's your coat? Aren't you cold?"

She hugged herself and shivered. "Oh yes, brrr," she said. "Must have forgotten it in my car."

"We can go get—"

"No no," she interrupted. "I think we'd both prefer to get this over with as soon as possible."

Stan nodded.

"A-sap," she said, then giggled a dreamy, girlish giggle.

"Okay," said Stan. It was his turn to shiver.

He held the door for her to enter the bar. She curtsied as she passed.

Bar None was busy for a Monday. It was full of the usual: a couple grabbing a late-night snack, a smattering of young hipsters, and a few frat boys getting wasted on cheap drinks at the bar. The angry-faced bartender nodded at Stan from in front of the mirrored wall of liqueurs. Stan waved. The bartender winked when he saw the woman.

The woman—Stan realized he still didn't know her name—took a look around, then hurried to the back of the bar. She sidled into a booth, and drummed her fingers on the tabletop. Stan sat across from her.

"I haven't caught your name," he said.

"Dalla," she said. She continued to tap her fingers.

Her gaze flicked from the front door, to the ceiling, to the bar, to the back door.

"Are you all right?" asked Stan.

"I don't like public places." She took a deep breath, then turned to Stan.

Dalla was pretty in the same way that Bloody was cute. Her stunning blue—nearly gray—eyes were too big for her face. Her bulb-tipped nose didn't go with her pointed cheekbones. Her lips formed a tight, thin gash on her face. Still, the overall package wasn't entirely unpleasant. Stan had slept with worse.

"Dalla. Let me get you a drink." He started to stand.

"No," she said. "I don't drink alcohol." She pulled an envelope and a pen from a beaded purse.

"Wait, first, tell me what happened. What happened to the couple you ran over? I know, I know, it must be difficult to talk about, but it's been eating at me since that day,"

For the first time since entering the bar, her thin lips curled into a smile. "Oh, them? No don't fret, it's nothing, they're fine." She swished her hand back and forth. "Just peachy. Walked away with barely a scratch."

"But I saw—" The bartender arrived beside their table.

"Stan," said the wiry red-haired man. "What's the what my friend?"

"Just keepin' on keepin' on," said Stan as he shook the man's hand. He introduced Dalla, then ordered a gin and tonic. The thought of more beer made him queasy.

"Oh, a drink you say?" said Dalla when he asked her what she wanted. "Bring me a soda; Coca Cola, I suppose."

When the bartender left, Stan leaned over the table.

"I saw blood," he whispered sternly. "And do you know who those people were?"

She broke into a grin. "David Letterman. It was an absolute delight to meet him; nicest fellow you could imagine. The young woman he was with, well, I wasn't as fond of her. I'm sure you're aware of who she was? So you can understand why he's chosen to keep the whole bang-up hush-hush?"

Stan thought about it for a moment. It was plausible enough, but he couldn't shake the memory of that lifeless hand flopped beside the car.

"Poor man is still quite rattled, I imagine," she said with some concern, though the corners of her lips remained curled. "Won't be able to host the show for a short while."

Whether Letterman was alive or dead was of no real consequence. Well, unless Stan could sell the last pictures of him alive. Come to think of it, maybe he could do it all anonymously. Go through the back channels. It wouldn't net as much cash, but anything would be better than living off of cold pizza in his cold apartment.

Dalla stared at him while he was lost in his own

thoughts. She licked her thin lips. Stan shivered. He wasn't sure if he was more disturbed by the woman, or his own horrible thought process.

The drinks arrived. Stan downed half of his gin and tonic in one gulp. Dalla stirred her Coke with the straw.

"Dammit," said Stan. "I've got questions, but this is just … it's too fucked up. Just give me those papers."

She handed over the envelope. He took out half a dozen pages of dense text.

"It says that myself and the law are absolving you of any responsibility in the crash. I can't collect insurance without it. The second part absolves me of any responsibility for damage to your car."

"Wait a second," said Stan. "Shouldn't you be paying for my broken tail light? And," he rolled his head around on his shoulders. "My neck still hurts. I might have some hefty medical bills, lady."

She stared at him with those icy eyes. "Do we really want to have to go through all that?"

No. No of course not, he supposed, it was more trouble than it was worth.

Those eyes continued to glow in the corner of his vision as he read the papers. They followed his finger, moving back and forth across the page, as she stirred her drink.

"You need to read every detail." She sounded curious, rather than angry.

"Suppose I do."

She smiled, nodded. Damn. Maybe it was the gin talking, but if this whole situation wasn't so bizarre, she really would be pretty.

After Stan signed the forms, he motioned to the bartender. Dalla rummaged through her purse, digging for change to hand to the bartender one coin at a time. She pulled out a keychain and placed it on the table. A plastic fob—a mini picture frame—hung from the keychain. In the frame was a picture of Damien Fox, topless.

When the bartender had left, Stan gestured at the picture. "Hah, big Damien Fox fan are you?"

"Oh, him? Well, yes. I suppose I am embarrassed, that you have pointed that out." It was impossible to tell if she was blushing, with her cheeks already red. She laughed a high-pitched girlish giggle.

"Nothing to be embarrassed about. He's been People's sexiest man alive three years in a row, so you're in good company. Heck, I used to have a poster of Jessica Alba in my bedroom. I think I was in love. You know, before she got all pregnant and motherly."

She smiled. For once she seemed to be genuinely amused. She leaned close, over the table, as if she had a secret. Stan was beginning to suspect that she had many.

"I know something about Damien Fox," she said. She leaned back, a finger to her mouth, smirking.

Stan leaned forward. "What?"

"Promise you won't tell anyone?"

He crossed his fingers and held them up. "Promise."

She giggled. "Honey, it's hard to believe that a professional paparazzi won't tell."

"How did you kn—"

"I know lots of things." She sighed. "I'll tell you anyway, because …" She stirred her drink around more. She still hadn't taken a sip of it. "… because you seem sweet."

Stan felt his face get hot. He adjusted his glasses. He hadn't had a compliment from a woman in months. Years, maybe.

"You know how Hillary Miller disappeared after that greatest hits album?" she asked.

"Yes," said Stan. "But what does that have to do w—"

Dalla held up her hand. Stan shut his mouth.

"Everybody's talking, saying she holed herself up in a cabin in the woods to focus on her music. Work on her big comeback.

"Well," she said with a mischievous grin, "everyone is wrong. She's holed up, sure, but only because she got knocked up. By Damien Fox."

"She's pregnant?"

"All P.G."

"Why would she hide that?"

"To avoid people like you. This is Damien's child, and Miller is a fine specimen of a young lady too, I suppose. You could say. Can you imagine how beautiful that child is going to be?" She fanned herself with the envelope full of forms. An ice cube in her untouched drink crackled. "You media folks would kill for a piece of it, wouldn't you? They won't be able to take the child to swim class without a swarm of photographers buzzing behind them."

"How do you know this?"

"Got myself a computer a few weeks ago. Did you know, on the world wide web, there are entire communities devoted to Damien Fox? Communitiesss," she hissed. "More than one. Hundreds of people gathering for no other purpose than to discuss his every move. Found the address of one of Damien's acting buddies, so I gave him a visit. He ended up spilling the beans. I can be quite convincing."

"I noticed. So where is the happy couple holed up then?" Stan could practically hear the cha-ching of the cash he could net if she were telling the truth.

She lowered her head and out came that disconcerting giggle. "Doozy of a question, Stanley Lightfoot. That is not something he told even his closest friends."

"Convenient," he said. He forced out a chuckle. "Well lady, it's quite the story, but I gotta get some sleep." He stood to leave.

Dalla was on her feet. "You don't believe me," she said, glaring at him with those eyes.

"Doesn't matter if I do or not," he said, but already he was trying to remember how much signed Damien Fox merch went for on eBay. Just in case.

He waved goodbye to the bartender, then walked

away. Dalla followed silently, close behind him. He swore he could feel her breath on the back of his neck. He zipped up his coat, then crossed the street to the door of his apartment building. When he turned around, Dalla was inches from his face. Her eyes bored into him. Her tongue caressed her thin lips.

"Invite me up for a cup of tea?"

Every fibre of Stan's being told him to call it a night, go to bed, and never see the bizarre woman again. Every fibre except the ones in his penis.

"Okay," he said.

❧

He paused outside his apartment. He could hear Bloody sniffing at the other side of the door.

"It's kind of a mess in there."

"Oh!" she said. "Oh, no worries, hun. I can't very well judge you; you've already outed me as a crazy ninny who obsesses over a celebrity."

"Guess we're not so different then. Hey thanks for telling me all that, even though you already knew, you know, what I do for a living."

He got out his keys. His hands were shaking. He hadn't been with a woman in a long time, and she seemed to be—what? Flirting? He couldn't really be sure what was going on in her head.

She smiled at him. He pushed his glasses up on his nose, tried to smile back, then turned to unlock the door. It took a few tries to get the trembling key in the lock. "You know, I wasn't sure what to make of you at first," he babbled. "Kinda thought you might even be, you know, dangerous."

"Oh, honey," she said, her breath on his neck. "Dangerous doesn't even begin to describe me."

He turned his head. Those eyes, those lips, they were inches from his.

Suddenly, she tossed her purse halfway down the hallway.

"Why did you—" he began.

"It's Michael Kors. Don't want to get blood on it."

Her teeth were buried in the side of his neck. A trickle of heat ran down the back of his shirt.

As he fell into her grip, he kicked against the door to throw her off balance. Instead, the door swung open. Bloody was a streak of grayish fur, then she clamped on the woman's leg.

"Get her," he said weakly. He felt weak, his muscles refusing to work, as if he'd just woken from a long nap.

Dalla unclenched her jaw and pulled away, her mouth dripping with blood that looked black in the flickering blue light. A quartet of fangs, two in the top and two in the bottom, occupied most of her mouth.

She stooped to wrench Bloody from her leg. When her grip momentarily weakened, Stan toppled forward, then scrambled into his apartment. "C'mon, Bloody, c'mon," he mumbled.

She tossed the dog against the wall. Bloody yelped

in pain and hit the floor with a thud. Dalla made to stomp on her with an ugly purple high-heeled shoe, but Bloody sprung to her feet. She deked one way, then the other, avoiding the foot coming down on her. A gray streak again, she was between Dalla's legs then in the apartment.

Stan slammed the door. He flicked the deadbolt and fastened the chain. Gripping his stinging neck, he stumbled across the apartment, collapsed on the couch, and reached for the phone beside it. His arms felt incredibly heavy.

He had time to dial 9 before the door was kicked in. He rolled off the couch just in time to avoid the door, torn from its hinges, crashing down half on the couch, half on the table beside it. There was a faint bong from underneath as the telephone smashed to pieces.

Bloody ran to cower by Stan's side. Silhouetted by the fluorescent hall lights, Stan's blackish blood splattered down the front of her flowery dress, the vampire crouched, hissing like an animal.

END OF PREVIEW

The full novel is available in most online stores, or here:
http://forestcitypulp.com/books/stars-and-other-monsters-by-phronk/

Made in the USA
Coppell, TX
04 January 2022

70894668R00080